"Dex, wait! Haven't you forgotten something? Your ring."

"Keep it," he said bitingly. "A memento of a failed affair. Unless, of course, you want to pay for it in kind. Unlike the dozens before me, I still have not seen your bedroom."

This mocking cynicism was the last straw. Flinging the ring at him, she yelled, "Get out! Go, go!"

"No one tells me to leave," he stated softly.

"Until now," she shot back.

"Never ever," he drawled quietly. "And certainly not a devious little girl like you, who doesn't know whether she wants to jilt me or jump me. I think we really need to know the answer, Bethany. Don't you?"

JACQUELINE BAIRD began writing as a hobby when her family objected to the smell of her oil painting, and she immediately became hooked on romance. She loves traveling and worked her way around the world from Europe to the Americas and Australia, returning to England to marry her teenage sweetheart. She lives in Northumbria, the county of her birth, and has two grown sons.

Books by Jacqueline Baird

HARLEQUIN PRESENTS®
1876—RAUL'S REVENGE
1915—MISTAKEN FOR A MISTRESS
1942—THE RELUCTANT FIANCÉE

JACQUELINE BAIRD

Giordanni's Proposal

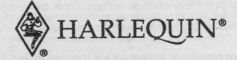

HARLEQUIN®

TORONTO • NEW YORK • LONDON
AMSTERDAM • PARIS • SYDNEY • HAMBURG
STOCKHOLM • ATHENS • TOKYO • MILAN • MADRID
PRAGUE • WARSAW • BUDAPEST • AUCKLAND

ISBN 0-373-12029-X

GIORDANNI'S PROPOSAL

First North American Publication 1999.

CHAPTER ONE

'No, NO, *nein, nada, non.* Is that clear enough for you, Mike? Or do I have to spell it out? N-O.'

'Don't be so negative, Beth, darling,' Mike drawled, his blue eyes dancing with amusement. 'You know you'll have fun, you always do with me.'

Beth stared down at her stepbrother in exasperation, but a hint of a smile pulled at the corners of her wide mouth. He really was the limit. Sprawled in her one and only comfortable chair, with one long leg draped over the arm, negligently swinging an expensively shod foot, he was the epitome of casual male elegance. The price of his shoes would have kept her for a month, she thought wryly. But that was Mike: handmade shoes, Savile Row suits, nothing but the best would do. Image was everything, according to Mike.

'Much as I love you, Mike, I am not going to dress up as a French tart to your *matelot* and let you throw me around the boardroom of Brice Wine Merchants, even if, according to you, the firm is celebrating its centenary and the chairman's birthday, and whatever else you care to tag on. The answer is still *no.*'

'But, Beth, I have a two-hundred-pound bet with my boss, the marketing director. He said I wouldn't dare liven up the chairman's party with an impromptu cabaret. Of course, I said I would, and I can't afford to lose.' He glanced up at her, his blue eyes narrowing assessingly on her lovely face. 'Unless, of course, you lend me the two hundred quid.'

'Oh, no! No way! Lending money to you is the equivalent of throwing it down the drain. You made the bet; you get out of it. Or, better still, why not ask one of your numerous girlfriends?'

'Ah, well, there's the rub... For the past six months I've concentrated exclusively on one particular, lovely girl.' His handsome face took on the expression of a love-sick puppy dog, much to Beth's astonishment. 'Elizabeth is the perfect woman for me. She is beautiful, intelligent and wealthy, and I fully intend to marry her one day. But unfortunately, when I suggested the wheeze to her, she told me to grow up and act responsibly, hence my throwing myself on your mercy.'

Mike in love... That Mike was contemplating marriage was mind-boggling. 'You really want to marry the girl?' Beth asked incredulously.

'Yes, more than anything else in the world.'

There was no doubting his sincerity; it was in his eyes, the unusual seriousness of his tone, the way he straightened up in the chair, before continuing, 'Which is why I daren't take the chance of asking another girl. If Elizabeth found out it would be curtains for me. She's very strong on fidelity. But as you're my stepsister, even if the joke does get out, she might be mad for a while, but at least she'll know I wasn't unfaithful.'

Then Beth did smile. This was typical of Mike's convoluted logic: it never occurred to him for a moment to forget the whole stupid idea. She remembered the first time she had met him. Home for Beth and her mother had been a small cottage in the village of Compton, not far from Torquay in Devon. Her late father had been an artist who'd never quite made it big before he died tragically young of a cerebral haemorrhage. Her mother also considered herself an artist, but in truth was a run-of-the-mill singer, who, between marrying men, craved fame. The summer Beth had met Mike, her mother had been performing in the summer season cabaret at a local theatre in Torquay. It was at the theatre that Leanora had met Ted, Mike's father. He'd been a widower and the agent of the star of the show.

After a whirlwind romance her mother and Ted had decided to marry. Beth, at eight, had been dressed up as a flowergirl in satin and lace, while Mike, at twelve, was supposed to be an usher. After a civil ceremony performed by a registrar they had, along with about a hundred guests, all descended on Torquay's largest hotel for the wedding breakfast.

During the reception Mike had crept under the top table unseen, except by Beth, and had tied the groom and the best man's shoelaces together. When the best man stood up to speak, the groom had been tipped backwards off his chair, and, as his arm was around his new bride at the time, Leanora had gone flying as well.

Thinking about it now could still bring a smile to Beth's face, and the four years that their parents had been a couple had probably been the happiest of Beth's childhood. They'd divorced when she was twelve, and Beth had spent the rest of her formative years at a convent boarding school, but Mike had always kept in touch; his letters and the few holidays they'd shared had been some of the brightest spots in her otherwise pretty miserable teenage years.

Which was why, she thought wryly three days later, as she stepped into the elevator of the Brice building at six o'clock on a Friday evening, she was about to make a fool of herself for the umpteenth time. Because of Mike...

'It is not too late to change your mind, Mike.' She cast an imploring glance at the man standing beside her. He was dressed in a long trenchcoat, as Beth was herself, perfectly suitable attire for an overcast October day in London. But the black beret perched at a flamboyant angle on his fair head looked decidedly odd.

'Stop worrying. It'll be fine. I've arranged with Miss Hardcombe, the Chairman's secretary, to start the music as we walk in the door. We throw off our coats and go into a one-minute routine, the same one we did for the school concert, and hey, presto, it's over! I am two hundred pounds better off, plus I score Brownie points with my boss for imaginative thinking.'

'But it's ten years since we last danced together at that school concert! We were just children, and still young and stupid enough to think we were going to be showbiz stars, for heaven's sake! We should have at least practised. I am bigger, slower and terrified,' Beth cried as the elevator door slid back.

It went fine at first. There were a few raised eyebrows as they entered the boardroom, but as bottles of wine and glasses littered the large table it was obvious a celebration was in progress, and Beth felt slightly reassured. A few grins made by the dozen men present, when Mike wished the chairman a happy birthday, did not bother her, and then the music started.

But when they slid off their coats the grins changed to chuckles, and Beth realised straight away she was at a distinct disadvantage. Whereas Mike looked reasonably decent, in tight black flared-bottom trousers and a navy and white striped sailor's jumper, she as the only woman present, looked outrageous, in a tiny black Spandex skirt, a red, scoop-neck clinging knit sweater and red stiletto-heeled shoes.

Worse was to follow, as Mike curved an arm around her waist and swung her round and away from him. She was supposed to let her feet slide along the floor, but unfortunately they had not counted on a thick-pile carpet, and her heel stuck. The chuckles turned to outright laughter. Then, when Mike picked her up and spun her around his head, to enthusiastic shouts of 'Bravo!', he got carried away and spun her around and around, until when he finally let go she was so dizzy she fell smack on her behind, her legs waving in the air.

Dazedly she looked up at the circle of sombre-suited men laughing down at her. Except that one of the men wasn't laughing. He stood slightly back from the rest, and, from her position on the floor he looked enormous. She tilted back her head and her green eyes clashed with a pair of icy grey.

He was the most compellingly attractive man in the room. How had she not noticed him before? Mesmerised, she stared up at him as he slowly shook his head, a stray curl of black hair flopping over his broad forehead. He arched one dark brow in a look that managed to be both entrancing and insulting before, making no effort to hide his boredom and contempt, he deliberately turned his back on her.

Arrogant devil, she thought furiously. But still her eyes lingered on his wide back, and his long, long legs, and she had the oddest feeling she had met him before. Impossible—he was not the kind of man any woman with a red corpuscle left in her body would ever forget. The word 'macho' could have been invented for this man. Also 'tough', 'uncompromising'... Beth's lips twitched. And with a gorgeous tight bum, she noted on a more basic note.

Suddenly, instead of looking at his back, she was staring once more at his front, at a rather indelicate level. She swallowed hard and jerked her head back, lifting her eyes to his face, and she had to swallow again at the transformation in his expression.

His hard mouth was curved in a wickedly sexy smile. 'Allow me,' he said in a deep velvet voice, and held out a very large hand.

Blushing to the roots of her hair, Beth grabbed the hand he offered and scrambled to her feet. She barely heard the numerous congratulations from the rest of the guests, or Mike's moment of triumph. Her whole attention was on the man before her.

Flushed and dishevelled, she had no idea how gorgeous she looked. She wasn't a conventionally beautiful woman, like her statuesque, elegant mother—for a start, Beth was only five feet two—but there was quite a lot else about her that was memorable. She had big eyes of a deep jade-green, a generously curved mouth and thick, naturally curly auburn hair, which had now sprung from the band holding it in check to riot around her small face in a rosy cloud. Unfortunately she also had a rather large bust that was in imminent danger of popping out of her top.

'Thank you,' she muttered, finally finding her voice, stumbling a little, scarlet with embarrassment. With her free hand she hastily adjusted her top, while her other hand stayed clasped in his much larger one. She looked up into his grey eyes and wondered how she had ever thought they were icy—now they were luminous, almost silver, and glittering with obvious appreciation. And his flashing smile was enough to make her want to collapse at his feet again.

'My pleasure. It isn't every day I get to rescue such a beautiful damsel in distress.'

He had said she was beautiful, and her own eyes widened in wonder as she drank in the sight of him. 'Tall, dark and handsome' did not do him justice. He was lethally attractive; he radiated a raw, primitive power that was unmistakable. Even in her bemused state she noted everyone had stepped back and given him space, as if it was his due.

'You all right, Beth?' She vaguely registered Mike's belated query.

'The lady is fine. I will take care of her,' the deep slightly accented voice responded curtly. But his gaze never left Beth's small figure, and, stooping slightly, he added, 'If that is all right with you, Beth. I may call you Beth?'

He could call her anything he liked, she thought stupidly, as long as he kept holding her hand and smiling down at her as if he had just discovered the crown jewels. 'Yes, yes, of course,' she murmured, enthralled by the wayward black curl that fell over his broad brow.

He squeezed her hand and slipped his other arm around her tiny waist. 'You look none too steady in those very dangerous shoes,' he said, justifying his familiarity as his silver gaze slid over her small face and lower, to her breasts, and on down to her feet, still encased in the ridiculously high-heeled shoes, and then back up to her face.

Beth was suddenly flushed with a totally different kind of heat. The warmth of his arm around her waist and the obvious admiration in his lazy gaze did weird things to her pulse-rate. What was happening to her? She had never reacted so instantly to a man in her life before. She had an overpowering urge to put her small hand on his broad chest, to run her fingers up the lapel of his immaculately tailored dove-grey suit, and to curl her fingers in the silky black curls that caressed the nape of his tanned neck. She lifted her hand, and gasped; she had almost done it…!

'I need a drink,' she blurted, and forced herself to step back. 'It's all right; I'm steady now,' she added, breaking free from his hold.

'You might be, but I don't think I will ever be again,' he husked, his silver eyes capturing hers. 'Don't move and I'll get you a drink.'

She couldn't have moved if she'd wanted to, her gaze following him as he turned and walked to the table, filled a fluted glass with amber liquid and turned back to offer it to her. She took it from him, the light brush of his fingers against hers sending a tremor up her arm that made her almost drop it. She took a hasty gulp of champagne, anything to hide her ridiculous reaction to him, but she had an uncanny feeling she would be unable to hide anything from this man, and yet she didn't even know his name.

'Who are you?' she asked, and was instantly horrified at her own bluntness.

'My friends call me Dex, my enemies, the bastard Giordanni. My mother christened me Dexter Giordanni. Dexter meaning, ''on the right hand''—possibly to compensate for my being born, on the ''left-hand side of the blanket.'' So take your pick.' He laughed at the look of shock on her lovely face.

'You're very blunt, Dex,' she said, stunned at his intimate revelation about his birth, but she could not help grinning back.

'So we are friends. Yes?'

'Yes.'

'In that case, can I take you out to dinner tomorrow night?'

'Tomorrow night,' she repeated, completely bowled over by his charm and obvious desire to see her again.

'Unfortunately this evening I have to dine with the chairman and his wife.' He gestured with his hand to where the head of the firm stood talking to Mike and a few others. Then, taking a card from his inside pocket, he said, 'Give me your address and phone number, and I will pick you up tomorrow night at seven-thirty. Okay?'

She hesitated, torn between the desire to say yes and her more cautious self, which reminded her that this man was a stranger who could be dangerous to her state of mind. He had already dented her ability to think straight simply by his presence. She looked at him with puzzled green eyes, and felt the tension simmer in the air between them.

He straightened up, squaring his wide shoulders. 'Unless, of course, your dancing partner has a prior claim to your time,' he added, in a voice that was suddenly hard.

'Mike?' she chuckled. 'You've got to be joking! He's my stepbrother. You don't really imagine I would make a fool of myself before a room full of strangers except with a member of the family? And, even so, I'm going to strangle the man when I get the chance.'

Dex's responding chuckle relieved the inexplicable tension between them. 'Good. So how about that address, please,' he pleaded huskily. 'I can see Brice heading this way.'

Beth looked around, and sure enough the chairman was walking towards them. 'All right.' In moments she had rattled off her address and telephone number.

Dex put the card back in his breast pocket just as the chairman arrived at his side.

Beth glanced at the man; not as tall as Dex, and quite a lot older, with a shock of white hair, he was still a very impressive figure.

'Thank you, young lady. You and Mike certainly enlivened the proceedings. That boy will go far.'

Beth blushed again, and mumbled her thanks, but the man had already turned to Dex. 'Sorry, Dexter, old chap, but I must drag you away from this very attractive young lady. My wife is expecting us at seven-thirty, and it is quite a drive.'

'Yes, of course, Brice,' Dex responded smoothly. And, as another man caught the chairman's attention for a moment, he leaned towards Beth and, in a quick aside, added, 'You've made quite an impression on Brice. Like older men, do you?' he asked with a smile, but the edge of cynicism in his tone was unmistakable.

She looked uncertainly into his grey eyes. Was he teasing or what? But before she could answer Brice cut in.

'Come on, Dex. I daren't keep my wife waiting.'

'Certainly, Brice.' Dex straightened to his full height and, slanting Beth a quick glance, confirmed, 'Seven-thirty, don't forget. But in case you do, I will ring tomorrow to remind you,' before turning on his heel and walking away with the chairman.

Beth followed him with her eyes; his dark head was bent towards the older man and he was seemingly deep in conversation with him as they exited the room. She let out her breath on a long sigh. She doubted if she really would see Dex again, and common-sense told her she would probably be better off without him.

Glancing around the room, she spotted her coat; someone had kindly placed it over a chair for her. The party seemed to be turning into some kind of stag night, with little appreciation of the fine wines on offer; it was more a case of who could down the most. There was nothing for her here. Crossing the room, she picked up her coat and pulled it on, wrapping it firmly around her.

Finally she spotted Mike near the door, and on her way out she collared him and hissed in his ear, 'I'm leaving you to your booze-up! But don't think I've forgotten. You owe me, and you owe me big for this, buster.'

'Hey, you should be thanking me. You've only pulled one of the wealthiest bachelors around. I heard him ask you out.'

The one trouble with auburn hair, she thought wryly, was the inevitable tendency for blushes to form on the pale complexion that went with it. 'Mr Giordanni? You know him?' She hesitated, torn between the desire to escape and the desire to hear more about Dex.

'Know him, sis? Not exactly, but I've heard of him. Everyone has. In the past ten years he has built up a huge business empire—he dabbles in everything, though there are some funny rumours as to how he got started. I know he owns a shipping line, and a string of hotels all over the globe—a couple of them here in London. Brice is hoping to get the contract to supply his hotels with liquor. Apparently, Giordanni has also just bought the Seymour Club in London—his reason for being here, I expect. His main home is somewhere in Italy, I believe.'

The more Mike talked, the more despondent Beth became. Dexter Giordanni was right out of her league, and she would be a fool to think otherwise.

'Okay Mike, forget it.' She tried to smile. 'I'm off. Enjoy your night.' And she left.

For a brief moment in time she had thought she had

met the man of her dreams. Who was she kidding? Love at first sight was a myth, and in any case things like that never happened to Beth—except in her fantasies!

Once more in the safety of her own apartment, Beth vowed for the hundredth time that never again would she get involved in Mike's hare-brained schemes. As for Mr Giordanni, obviously he had simply been flirting with the only woman around at the time, and would never give her a second thought. Beth dismissed him from her mind. She would never see him again.

She showered and changed into a soft towelling robe, then curled up in the solitary armchair and sighed with pure contentment. Alone at last. Funny, as a child she had longed to be a part of a large family. Her own father had died when she was two and she had no memory of him. Her first stepfather had not lasted past her sixth birthday, when her mother, Leanora, had divorced him, and Beth had very little memory of him either.

Then had come Mike and his father, the lovely house on the English Riviera, overlooking the bay in Torquay and for a few years Beth had felt part of a family. Until her mother had decided a young actor suited her better and had divorced Mike's dad to marry her toy-boy. Then she'd stuck Beth in a boarding school and taken off on tour.

For once, her mother had been the one to suffer when, a year later, the young man had divorced her. But nothing stopped her mother for long, though, Beth thought dryly, stirring in her seat. Three years ago, Leanora had married an Australian cattle rancher. The poor man had been visiting Devon to trace his ancestors when Leanora had convinced him he needed a wife. Beth had never even met Leanora's fifth husband—technically her stepfather.

After the fiasco this afternoon, she had reached the conclusion that there was a great deal to be said for being an orphan. Without family to get her into trouble, life was a joy…

But later a little imp of mischief whispered in her head as she curled up in her cosy bed and tried to sleep. An even greater joy might be hers if the outrageously attractive Italian Dexter Giordanni actually turned up tomorrow night to take her out to dinner. With his handsome face clear in her mind's eye, she fell asleep, the eroticism of her dreams a testament to the earth-shattering effect he had had upon her.

CHAPTER TWO

BETH eyed the pile of laundry with a wry grimace.
Saturday was her day for washing, cleaning the apartment and shopping—always in that order. Usually she
enjoyed having the weekend to herself, but today she
felt oddly restless. With a sigh, she picked up the gar-
ments and shoved them in the washing machine. Turning
it on to the correct setting, she decided to break with
habit and do her shopping immediately—not for a second admitting she wanted to get out and back quickly
just in case Dexter Giordanni telephoned.

By late afternoon, her apartment spotless, her clothes
dried and ironed, she was beginning to regret turning
down her friend Mary's offer to go to the cinema with
her. She had a sinking feeling her Saturday night was
going to be spent alone in front of the television, and it
was her own stupid fault. A man like Dexter Giordanni
was not going to call the likes of her in a million years...

Still, she might as well shower and wash her hair; she
had nothing else to do. And with that thought in mind
she stripped off her jeans and shirt in the bedroom and
padded to the bathroom. The ringing of the telephone
had her sprinting back to the kitchen like an Olympic
runner.

She snatched the receiver off the wall. 'Yes?' she said
breathlessly.

'I hope I did not disturb you,' the deep, dark voice
echoed down the line.

If only he knew, Beth thought, grinning to herself. Just

the sound of his voice disturbed her more than any other man she had ever known... 'No, no, not at all. I was just about to step in the shower,' she told him truthfully.

'Ah, the image is *incantevole*, but I must not delay you. I simply called to confirm our dinner date: seven-thirty, yes?'

'What does *incant*...whatever mean?' Beth asked, diverted by his lapse into his native language.

'Enchanting... *Ciao*.' And he replaced his receiver.

Beth stood holding the telephone for a long moment. Dex thought she was enchanting. Taking a deep, contented breath, she replaced her receiver and dreamily made her way back to the bathroom.

An hour later, wearing only a towel, Beth stood in front of her open wardrobe and viewed its contents with a jaundiced eye. Her date would be here in twenty minutes and she had nothing to wear. Apart from a couple of tailored suits she wore for work, the rest of her clothes were all casual. She was very much a jeans and sweater sort of girl, and somehow the red wool shirt-dress she kept for special occasions looked far too plain. Why, oh, why hadn't she spent the afternoon shopping for an elegant, sophisticated dress to match the sophisticated Dex, instead of lolling around her apartment?

She glanced across the room to the window. The weather hadn't changed; it was still a grey, cold, overcast autumn evening, and with a resigned sigh she took her only sophisticated dress out of the wardrobe. She had bought it in July for her graduation ball. A simple black satin slip dress, it had a delicate gold thread shimmering though it, tiny shoestring straps, a scooped neck and back and an A-line skirt that ended a few inches above her knee. She dropped it on the bed and turned back to the wardrobe. The frock was fine, but she would be freezing in today's weather.

Unlike some young woman of her age, who quite happily went out in all weathers with arms and legs bare, Beth was thoroughly sensible, and not prepared to get pneumonia for the sake of fashion. So reluctantly she dragged from the top shelf of a wardrobe a plain black wool shawl, a purchase from one of the high street chains, and threw it on the bed.

She crossed the room, opened the chest of drawers and withdrew a pair of delicate black lace panties and matching garter belt. Dropping the towel to the floor, she quickly pulled on her underwear, then, lifting the dress from the bed, slid it over her head. Cut on the bias, it was too low at the back to allow the wearing of a bra. But, eyeing her reflection in the mirror, she thought, not bad!

Sitting down at the dressing table, she quickly applied a moisturiser to her fine skin. She took a little longer than usual over her eye make-up, accentuating her large eyes with the merest hint of pale aquamarine eyeshadow at the corners and a fine line of brown kohl around the top lid, finishing off with brown-black mascara to enhance her long thick lashes. A gloss of natural pink for her lips, and she was almost ready.

She picked up her hairbrush and brushed her auburn curls vigorously. Then, with a deft twist, she piled her hair on the top of her head, securing it with a discreetly coloured band, and finished off by pushing a few strategic curls firmly in place.

Satisfied with the result, she stood up, and from the dressing table drawer removed a pair of fine black nylon stockings. Carefully pulling them on one by one, she clipped the small black suspenders in place and, straight-

ening, smoothed her skirt down over her thighs. She
turned to look over her shoulder at her image: no bumps
or brief line! Good.

She slipped her feet into classic black patent leather
pumps with two-and-a-half-inch heels. She needed the
height, she reminded herself, before taking a small black
patent clutch purse from the dressing table and quickly
transferring a few essentials from her everyday shoulder
bag.

The doorbell rang, disturbing the silence and panicking Beth. She grabbed the black shawl from the bed and
slung it around her shoulders before dashing out of the
bedroom to the front door. She pressed the button for
the intercom and heard that familiar rich voice.

'Giordanni, here.'

'I'll be right down,' she responded. For some reason
she was not quite ready to ask him into her home.

The elevator deposited her in the foyer, and when she
saw him leaning indolently against the porter's desk,
dressed in an immaculately fitting black dinner suit with
a white silk shirt and perfectly knotted black velvet bow
tie, her heart skipped a beat. Suddenly she had a vivid
image of herself untying the bow tie and running her
fingers over the broad expanse of chest, and she wished
she had asked him up to her apartment. She caught her
breath at the uncharacteristic erotic thought.

Consequently she blushed fire-engine red when,
straightening to his full height, he strolled across and
quite naturally took her arm, and looked down at her.

'I was right, you look enchanting. Shall we go?'

Her, 'Hello, Dex,' was greeted with the briefest of
slanting smiles before he was ushering her out of the
door and into a chauffeur-driven limousine.

'I don't keep a car in London. I am not here that often,

and when I am I use a rental service. So I hope you don't object to a driver this evening, Beth. Plus, I thought we might celebrate our meeting with a few glasses of champagne, and I never drink and drive.'

'A very laudable resolution,' she managed to say calmly. She cast him a sidelong glance, almost furtively. He was as devastatingly attractive as she remembered, and, sitting next to him in the close confines of the back seat of the car, with the pressure of his thigh lightly pressing against her own and the soft elusive scent of his aftershave teasing her nostrils—or maybe it was simply the scent of the man himself—she was completely overwhelmed by Dex, the car—everything.

A large hand closed over her small hands, which were clenched in her lap. 'Beth, really. "A laudable resolution"? My knowledge of your language is excellent, but what does that mean?' he asked with a chuckle, and lifted her hands to his lips so she was forced to look at him, his silver eyes glinting down into hers. 'Beth, I like you for your openness, your honesty. Don't go all stuffy on me now.'

The touch of his lips on her hand and the humour in his gaze excited her, but also calmed her nerves. If he wanted honesty he could have it, she thought, secretly pleased. 'You're right, Dex, "laudable" was a bit much. But you make me rather nervous. I've never been out with a man quite like you before, or sat in a chauffeur-driven limousine. It's quite awesome.'

He lowered her hands to her lap and gave them a gentle squeeze before letting go. 'You are not frightened of me, Beth, are you?' he asked softly, but before she could respond he added, 'You have no need to be. I have only your best interests at heart, and I am sure you will very soon get used to my great wealth and everything else; women usually do.'

Beth looked up, not all sure she liked his last comment, and thought she caught a flash of something very like cynicism in his eyes. But, realising she was watching him, Dex turned the full force of his megawatt smile on her small face and dropped a brief, swift kiss on her forehead.

'Don't look so worried, little one. Tonight we are going to have fun, I promise.'

The brief kiss banished all her doubts, and half an hour later, seated opposite Dex in the most exclusive restaurant in London, she wondered why she had worried. He was the perfect companion. Articulate, charming, Dex ordered the meal with an efficiency and knowledge of fine food Beth marvelled at. But he was not above making her laugh with his description of the waiter.

Very quickly he made her feel completely at ease, though every so often he very gently flirted with her, making her aware by a touch, a glance, of his purely masculine interest in her as a woman. Or maybe not so pure... Beth did not know, and she had not the experience to make a judgement.

They had exchanged snippets of information about themselves. Dex was thirty-three to her twenty-one. He knew she was a graphic artist, and she knew he was extremely wealthy, as he told her in great detail how many companies he owned. In fact, his wealth struck the one discordant note in her otherwise rapt fascination with the man.

'You're not one of those bleeding-heart radical types who object to a man being disgustingly rich, are you?' he asked jokingly.

For a second she felt his humour did not ring true. But, dismissing the uneasy thought with a toss of her head, she aimed for a sophisticated response.

'Not at all. Someone once said that no woman can be too rich or too thin, or something like that, and I'm inclined to agree.' She wasn't sure she meant what she had said, but it seemed to please Dex.

'Good girl! I knew the moment I saw you you were my type of woman,' he drawled, watching her with a gleam of satisfaction in his grey eyes.

Beth felt the colour rise in her cheeks. She was delighted he thought she was his type, but not absolutely sure if she had been complimented or insulted.

By the time the main course arrived Beth had just about got her chaotic emotions under control, and was actually beginning to feel as if she had known the man for years.

'Honestly, Dex, I don't think I'll be able to eat all this.' She eyed her duck and cranberry sauce. It looked delicious, but they had started with roasted asparagus salad, followed by a fish course—A trio of smoked fish with beetroot—and now, with the main course before her, she wondered if she would ever get through it all.

'Eat what you like and leave the rest. For myself, I am a big man with a big appetite. I intend to enjoy…' His silver eyes gleamed with blatant desire as they caught and held hers, then deliberately dropped to the soft valley of her breasts, delicately exposed by the neckline of her dress. 'Everything…' he husked, his gaze lifting to her face. 'It is the only way to live.'

Beth was not stupid, she knew what he meant, and she could feel the colour rising in her cheeks yet again, as her stomach clenched. She knew it had nothing to do with the food but everything to do with the potent appeal of the man opposite.

'Eat. I did not mean to embarrass you,' Dex offered quietly. 'But you have the most amazing effect on me. I look at you and I want you in my bed.'

Beth gasped out loud, and his eyes narrowed with piercing intensity on her flushed face.

'You know this is true, and you feel the same; don't try to deny it,' he commanded arrogantly, but then in a softer tone he added, 'But perhaps now is not the time to talk of such matters.'

She wanted to deny it. His supreme confidence was somehow insulting. But she knew what he said was true, so instead she contented herself with fiddling with her fork and asking, 'Are you always so blunt on a first date?'

'No,' he said, and, reaching across the table, he covered the hand holding her fork, 'Only with you, Beth.' Suddenly grinning, he added, 'So, tell me more about yourself. Your friends, parents, whatever. Talk to me, so I can take my mind off your luscious body and get back to my meal, hmm?'

He was impossible, but Beth found herself grinning back and doing exactly as he had said. 'Family—I don't have much. I don't remember my father; he died when I was a baby. I've spent most of my life in Devon with my mother. She had aspirations to be a famous singer, but unfortunately also a tendency to get married a lot. She is on her fifth husband now and lives in Australia. I haven't seen her for three years, though we do write occasionally.' Beth broke off, raised her glass to her mouth and took a gulp of champagne. She didn't really like talking about Leonora, and sometimes it still upset her, though she never liked to admit it.

'That explains a lot,' Dex murmured.

'Sorry, what did you say?' Lost in her own thoughts for a moment, she had missed his comment.

'That must have hurt a lot,' Dex repeated softly.

'No, not really,' she quickly assured him, comforted by the sympathy in his tone. 'I got used to it, and on the plus side I acquired a stepbrother—Mike. If it hadn't been for Mike I wouldn't have met you.' She stopped. The champagne was going to her head and she was revealing more than she meant to.

Dex, a smile curving his firm mouth, lifted his glass. 'A toast to a much-married mum and Mike, without whom you and I would never have met.'

Embarrassed, but oddly pleased, Beth lifted her glass and returned the toast. Replacing her glass on the table, she said, 'No more champagne; I think I've had quite enough.' And, pushing her almost empty plate slightly forward, she continued, 'No more food, either. It was delicious, but I really can't eat any more.'

'I don't have that problem,' Dex drawled, clearing his plate and placing the cutlery on it. 'In fact, I think I'll have a dessert; I love sweet things.' And, catching her green eyes with his, he continued throatily, 'You are the sweetest thing I have met in a long time. Can I have you, Beth?' Then, tossing his head back, he laughed out loud at her look of confusion.

She wanted to be offended but his laughter was infectious, so she smiled, then laughed as well. 'You know, I've discovered something about you, Dexter Giordanni,' she finally managed to say pertly. 'You are an incorrigible flirt.'

'Only with you, Beth, only ever with you.'

If only she could believe him, she thought, gazing at him as he paid the bill, adding a very generous tip. She

had been out with plenty of men—well, not plenty, more
like half a dozen. Her last date had been with a young
man from the office. She had spent an enjoyable evening
in a local wine bar with Dave, but they had both decided
without a word being spoken they were destined to be
workmates and nothing more. Now, watching Dex, she
knew this was different. She could very easily fall in
love with him, and it frightened her even as it excited
her.

He turned his head and caught her staring, and one
dark brow arched enquiringly. 'Have I got a smudge on
my nose?' he asked, perfectly aware she had been studying him.

'No, you have a very nice nose,' she shot back. 'I was
simply thinking what a lovely evening it has been.' That
was not exactly a lie, she told herself, rather proud of
her ability to appear cool and collected in his sophisticated presence, when inside her heart was beating like a
drum.

'Has been? But it is not over yet; the night has hardly
begun.' Getting to his feet, he took the shawl the waiter
handed to him. 'Come on, you look the sort of girl who
likes to take chances. I will show you my new casino.'

Beth stood up and smoothed her skirt down over her
slender hips, intensely aware of Dex's blatantly sensual
gaze following the movement of her hands as his own
large hands carefully slipped her wrap around her shoulders,

'You look beautiful,' he murmured, his hands lingering for a moment on her shoulders. His dark head bent
and his lips brushed the top of her head. 'Let's get out
of here before I make a fool of myself.' Slipping his
hand down to the small of her back, he guided her out
of the restaurant and into the waiting limousine.

Inside, seemingly casually, Dex curved his long arm
around her shoulders and pulled her swiftly close to him.
All Beth's hard-won poise deserted her in an instant,
and, looking up at him through the thick brush of her
lashes, she quivered at the glimpse of fire that blazed in
his eyes.

'You're safe with me, Beth,' he murmured softly.

'I know.' Beguiled by his many compliments and real
desire for her, she believed him, and snuggled into his
side with a deep sigh of contentment. The rest of the
trip was accomplished in a companionable silence until
the car stopped.

Sitting up, Beth glanced out of the window. 'Is this
it?' she said feeling rather disappointed. There were no
neon lights or flashing signs, simply an elegant black
and gold door in the centre of what looked like a typical
Georgian terraced house.

'Discretion is the name of the game,' Dex offered,
helping her out of the car. Taking her hand in his, he
led her across the pavement and through the black door
into another world.

As soon as they walked into the entrance foyer a
young woman dashed to take her wrap. Then a hard-
faced man appeared and Dex introduced her—the casino
manager, a Mr Black, a name Beth found very appropriate; he was swarthy, stocky, and looked dangerous
while his voice oozed charm.

She had never been in a casino before, but when Dex
ushered her into a huge room with a graceful curved
staircase leading to the upper floor it didn't take her long
to realise it was a very serious business. Glittering crys-
tal chandeliers illuminated a dozen or more tables surrounded by smartly dressed people. The walls were lined
with slot machines, like an army of alien, robotic guards,

with yet more people seated in front of them. But it was the avid expressions on the customers' faces that Beth found somehow chilling.

'You look a little stunned,' Dex opined, with a dry smile. 'Surely you have been in a casino before?'

'No, I haven't, and I can't believe so many people are prepared to waste money this way,' she said bluntly. Her answer seemed to surprise him, but not for long.

'Then you ain't seen nothing yet, babe,' he drawled in a mock-American accent. His grey gaze swept down over the soft curve of her breasts and back to her face, and with a seductive look, he added, 'Stick with me, babe, and I'll show you a good time.' And, putting an arm around her waist, he chuckled at her look of outrage.

'Fool,' Beth laughed, realising he was teasing, and gave him a sharp dig in the ribs with her elbow.

'I know, but I can't resist teasing you.' At that point Mr Black said something in Dex's ear, and the amusement left his face.

'Sorry, Beth, I need to go to the office, but I'll show you the rest on the way. This is just for starters. The bar and restaurant are through there.' He gestured with his free hand as they reached the bottom of a grand staircase. 'Up here there are two more gaming rooms, where the stakes rise accordingly. Plus the offices,' he informed her as they ascended the stairs, his arm dropping from her waist.

Beth watched him as they walked up, and saw a stranger. Dex was suddenly all efficiency, no trace of humour left. Tall and aloof, he strode up the stairs and through to another room, taking deferential greetings from various people with a word, or a nod, and a smile that never reached his eyes.

His plain black dinner suit and conservative white

shirt could not conceal the powerful muscled body beneath, or a certain air of danger about him. The other people in the room faded into insignificance beside him. It was obvious to Beth, and everyone else, that this man was the master of all he surveyed, the hard-headed, powerful ruler of the lot; the Boss. It wasn't just his height or his build, but the intangible aura he carried with him, a dynamism that radiated from him, a supreme confidence in his own worth that made weaker mortals shrink back.

Beth shuddered; a ghost is walking over my grave, she thought, but dismissed the notion when Dex halted her with a large hand curving over her shoulder. The touch of his hand on her bare flesh was enough to make her forget every rational thought.

His dark head bent towards her, and in her heightened emotional state she imagined he was going to kiss her, but she was sadly disillusioned when he said starkly, 'This room is for the high rollers, where the real money changes hands. Black is getting you some chips so you can play.'

Play! She wouldn't know where to start. Curious, Beth looked around: no slot machines here, but a peculiar silence, punctuated by the occasional voice of a croupier. Around the large green baize tables were expensively dressed customers, some obviously from the Middle East, judging by their garb, and the few ladies present, mostly old, wearing enough jewellery to pay off the National Debt.

'Here, Beth.' Dex thrust a handful of round tokens at her. 'Enjoy yourself. I won't be long.'

'Can't I come with you?' she blurted, suddenly feeling completely out of her element. 'I'm not a gambler, and I don't think I want to be.'

His fingers caught her chin and he tilted her head up. 'You look stunningly beautiful, Beth, and I will get my business concluded much quicker without you to distract me. Understand?' His grey eyes roamed over her delicate features. 'You will be perfectly all right on your own; no one will bother you.' His glance slid down her body like a warm caress, and back to her face again. 'Everyone knows you're with me,' he ended with unconscious arrogance, and, letting his hand slide from her chin to her shoulder, he squeezed her gently in a casual reassuring gesture.

'Yes...w-well,' she stuttered. Her flesh burned beneath his fingers and her body was aware of him with every pore.

She tore her gaze from his and glanced distractedly around the room. Her green eyes widened in astonishment as she caught sight of someone she knew—Paul. Even in this crowd he stood out.

Tall, his blond hair turning here and there to white, his exquisitely tailored dinner suit fitting his slim, elegant body to perfection, he looked what he was: a man of distinction. The lines of character in his face reflected his fifty-three years, but in no way detracted from his handsome features.

Paul Morris... He looked across, his blue eyes surprised when they met Beth's. She watched as he made his way towards her, determination in every stride. But he was supposed to be in Italy. What was he doing back so soon? she wondered. Her lips curled in a slow smile. At least she wouldn't be alone.

She glanced back at Dex, whose hand hadn't left her shoulder. 'Okay,' she said. But he was not looking at her, instead he was watching Paul approach, with a dark frown on his face.

'No, you are right. You are coming with me,' Dex ordered curtly, his hand dropping to her waist and hauling her hard against him.

'Bethany, what on earth are you doing here?' Paul stopped a foot away, and, taking in the proprietary arm around her waist, he flashed a hard smile at Dex. 'Giordanni. I'd heard you were buying the place. Congratulations.' Then, turning worried blue eyes back to Beth, he continued, 'I didn't know you knew Mr Giordanni, Bethany.'

'And I thought you were in Italy,' she shot back. She had dined with him ten days ago and he had told her he was going to his estate in Italy.

'Oh, I was, and I will be again in another few hours.' Paul glanced at the gold Rolex on his wrist. 'This is just a flying visit—twenty-four hours. I had some business that couldn't wait. That's why I didn't call you. But enough about me. What are you doing here? You don't gamble,' he ended sternly.

Beth opened her mouth to answer but was forestalled by Dex.

'The lady is with me, Morris.' His fingers nipped her waist, demanding her compliance. 'And we have urgent business to attend to in private—haven't we, darling?' Dex's grey eyes captured hers and his head lowered, his firm mouth brushing her parted lips. It was a fleeting kiss, but it was enough to set her heart racing, and she stared back at him, too dumb to answer.

'I hope you know what you're doing, Beth.' Paul said, bringing her back into the conversation.

She looked at Paul and smiled a misty, bemused smile. 'Yes, Paul.'

Paul sighed, a wry smile of acceptance curving his

mouth. She was a grown woman; it had to happen some time.

'You're a man of the world, Morris, I'm sure you understand,' Dexter cut into the silence. 'Enjoy your gambling and excuse us.' And with a deft twist Dexter spun Beth round.

She only had time to call, 'See you, Paul,' over her shoulder as, with almost indecent haste, Dex urged her towards the back of the room and a large nondescript door. The incongruous note was the man who guarded it and opened it at their approach. He looked like a heavyweight boxer with the nose to match.

She registered that they were in a dimly lit hallway, and had opened her mouth to ask where the fire was— she would have quite liked to talk to Paul—when she registered the stark fury in Dex's steely eyes.

'Old man Morris a friend of yours, is he?'

'Yes, a very good—' She never got the chance to finish the sentence.

Dex pushed her back against the wall, his dark head swooping down, his mouth capturing hers in a kiss of pure male dominance. Shocked by his sudden aggression, the fierce pressure of his mouth, the feel of his huge body hard against her much smaller frame, she instinctively struggled to break free. But she was helpless against his superior strength, and his mouth ground against hers with a demanding arrogance that was as exciting as it was alien to her.

Then, suddenly, something peculiar happened. One second she was fighting him and the next she felt her body melting against his as his lips gentled against her mouth. His kiss softened, his tongue traced the outline of her mouth, his teeth nibbled gently on her bottom lip until, with a sigh of complete surrender, she opened her

mouth to him. She lifted her hands, her fingers tangling
in the silky black thickness of his hair, and kissed Dex
back without realising what she was doing.

His mouth burned against hers, his tongue toying with
hers in an erotic, thrusting dance. Her hands slid to his
broad shoulders. She felt his muscles tense beneath the
smooth fabric of his jacket and trembled as his hand slid
down her naked throat, his long fingers tracing the soft
curve of her breast and palming its lush fullness in his
hand, before sliding lower, tracing the indentation of her
waist, the soft flare of her hips. It was only when she
felt his hand stroke up her leg to her naked thigh she
began to panic again. 'No.' Beth uttered a cry of protest
and closed her hand around his strong wrist.

Dex finally raised his head, his breathing surprisingly
unsteady. 'Stockings as well. What are you trying to do
to me?' he groaned as he slid his hand from under the
hem of her short dress and, drawing away from her,
brushed his ruffled hair from his brow. They stared at
each other, neither one capable of speech for a moment.
But it was Dex who recovered first.

'I guessed you would be dynamite, but I admit even
I am surprised at exactly how explosive we are together.'
His grey eyes glittered down into hers. She stared back,
her pulse thudding erratically, her green eyes wide and
bemused. She was so stunned by her own violent reaction, she couldn't speak.

'I was right; I should have left you to the gaming
tables. You are more than a distraction; you're a lethal
weapon, lady.' He grinned, a self-deprecating smile, and,
clasping her hand in his, he added, 'Come and I will
show you the rest of my newly acquired toys, before we
get into any more trouble.'

Beth was grateful for his matter-of-fact attitude; it

helped to calm her leaping responses. Then Mr Black appeared at the end of the hall and it was back to business for Dex. They left her sitting in a functional office and retired to an inner sanctum, Dex having explained that it was the manager's office and also the strongroom.

Beth spent the rest of their evening together in an emotional haze, trying to deal with her chaotic response to Dex. She was glad when, on returning to the outer office, he suggested taking her home. In the car he arranged to call for her the next morning at ten, and, on walking her to the door of her apartment, the light kiss he pressed on her lips was warm and somehow reassuring.

Tired, but happy, she crawled into bed, expecting to sleep. But she lay awake for hours, her mind reliving the events of the night. The intimate dinner with Dex, the sound of his deep, sexy voice, the touch of his hand. She tossed restlessly, her body unnaturally warm, her breasts hardening as she remembered the casino, and the sudden passionate interlude on the way to the office.

She turned over onto her stomach and buried her head in the pillow. Any more erotic memories, Beth told herself sternly, and she would never sleep. Closing her eyes, she tried to make her mind blank, but something niggled at her conscience until finally she remembered.

Dex had thrust the chips in her hand and told her to play. It had been odd... One minute he had been determined to leave her at the gaming tables, and yet he had changed his mind in a flash when she had spoken to Paul. Maybe Dex was jealous! Surely that proved he was as smitten with her as she was with him. On that happy notion, Beth drifted off to sleep.

CHAPTER THREE

BETH woke up to bright autumn sunshine blazing through the window, and she smiled to herself. It was an accurate reflection of how she felt inside, and all because Dexter Giordanni had entered her life... She said his name out loud as she jumped out of bed and headed for the shower, loving the sound of his name almost as much as she loved the man.

She froze, one foot in the shower stall; the enormity of what she had just admitted to herself hit her like a bolt from the blue. Slowly she stepped into the shower and turned on the water. The impossible had happened. She had fallen in love at first sight.

A worried frown creased her smooth brow. What was she thinking of? In love...she couldn't be. Beth had always prided herself on being sensible where men were concerned, and had never let a man get too close to her. The example of her mother, Leanora, had taught her from an early age that there was no such thing as true love. And watching her stepbrother's girlfriends come and go like yo-yos had confirmed Beth's cynicism where the L-word was concerned. Yet here she was, mooning like a love-sick calf over a man she had only just met.

Dex was an experienced man of the world. He probably knew exactly how he affected her. Who was she fooling? Not probably, positively! Beth blushed at the memory of being locked in his arms, his hand on her breast, her thigh. Abruptly she turned the water from hot to cold, and when she felt thoroughly numb she stepped out of the shower and rubbed herself down with a large towel with a lot more force than was strictly necessary— memories of her years in the convent school reminding her of the sins of the flesh.

Dried, and dressed in navy trousers, a white silk shirt and a buttercup-yellow wool cardigan, Beth ate her breakfast of cereal and toast. Lingering in the kitchen over her second cup of coffee, she told herself she must slow down where Dex was concerned. She had dressed conservatively, and she would act with reserve in his company today. She was frightened of how he could make her feel, and her innate common sense told her she hardly knew the man.

It was a much more subdued Beth who opened the door an hour later to the object of her turbulent thoughts.

'Don't I get a smile?' Dex demanded in a throaty drawl.

She had managed to stay calm long enough to say hello to him over the intercom and let him in to the building. But seeing him in the flesh knocked every sensible resolution out of her head. He was leaning with one arm propped against the doorframe, his large body almost blocking the light and angled towards Beth.

She couldn't help it. Her green eyes widened in fascinated appraisal of the man in front of her. 'Dark and dangerous' flashed through her mind. She had only seen him wearing a formal suit before, but this morning he was dressed in a black roll-neck sweater, and a black leather blouson jacket sloped off his broad shoulders. His faded blue jeans were verging on the indecent, slung low on his hips, with a leather belt threaded through the loops that Beth was sure was not necessary to hold them up. They fitted him like a second skin, hugging his long, long legs, with a tell-tale lighter patch in a more intimate place. Flushing furiously, she raised her eyes to his and went even redder.

His grey eyes gleamed with a mocking, sensuous delight. He knew exactly how his overt masculinity affected her. 'Are you going to ask me in, Beth, or am I supposed to stay here all day?'

'No, no...of course. Yes, yes, come in...' she prattled like a demented fool, stepping back and signalling with her hand for him to enter. His husky laugh simply added to her confusion.

He stood in the middle of her sitting room and slowly looked around. 'This is not at all what I expected,' he said, with a wry shake of his dark head.

It was her home, and immediately Beth was on the defensive. 'I've only lived here a couple of months, and it takes time and money to buy furniture and things.'

Beth looked around her living room, trying to see it through Dex's eyes. It was small—one corner was completely taken up with her computer and a large drawing board, another with the television and CD player. On the walls she had pinned a few of her favourite posters. Her one and only armchair, in battered black leather, stood next to an old wooden chest she had bought on the Portobello Road to use as a coffee table. The rest of the furniture consisted of three cheap and cheerful scarlet bean bags.

Dex stepped towards her, and, tilting her face up to his, with a finger under her chin, said, 'I did not mean to offend you. I love your decor. It is like you—bright and colourful.'

'Yes, well.' With his grey eyes smiling down into hers, she was almost lost for words.

'I was surprised by the drawing board; you really do

work as a graphic artist and obviously take your job seriously if you bring work home.'

'Not so much bring work home; I like to experiment with ideas on the computer and then transfer them to the bigger, more traditional board. I find I get a better view that way,' she replied, finally managing to string a reasonable sentence or two together.

'A better view.' Dex's hand fell from her chin and he glanced around the room again. 'That is a good idea; I must remember that,' he said enigmatically.

Beth watched him, an odd breathlessness afflicting her as his grey gaze captured hers. His dark head bent towards her, and for a second she had the impression he was going to kiss her. But, instead, he lifted his hand and brushed a stray wisp of her hair behind her ear.

'Unless you want to give me a guided tour of your bedroom, I suggest we leave.'

There was no mistaking the teasing gleam in his eyes, and Beth reciprocated in kind. 'I am quite sure you've never needed to be guided around any lady's bedroom in your life. Your type are born knowing the way.'

Dex chuckled, and then laughed out loud. 'You know me too well already. That makes you a dangerous lady,' he drawled in genuine amusement, and he was still grinning when they left the building and he helped her into the front passenger seat of a black BMW car.

The shared humour lasted. As he drove Dex regaled her with stories of some of the more colourful gamblers he had met at his casinos. She howled with laughter when he described an elderly lady tourist who had holidayed on one of his luxury liners cruising around the Mediterranean. Apparently, after visiting the island of Sicily, the lady, on returning to the ship, had been most indignant and insisted on complaining to the captain, because she had been told the volcano, Mount Etna was live, but it had not erupted while she was there.

Listening to him talk, Beth also realised he took his work very seriously. His head office was in Rome, where he spent most of the time, but he also made a point of trying to visit every hotel, cruise liner and casino he owned at least once a year. At present he was staying at his London hotel until his business in London was completed. He had an apartment in New York, but he preferred Italy, and Beth surmised his real home was Rome.

The information he freely offered about his lifestyle should have reassured her. But in fact it only underlined what she already knew. He was a sophisticated, dynamic business tycoon, and way out of the reach of a struggling graphic artist.

But, glancing sideways at him as the car sped out of the city and into the open countryside, Beth hoped she was wrong. She noted the slight frown lines between his eyes as he tried to read a signpost, and somehow he looked younger, not quite so self-assured. Maybe it was the casual clothes he wore, she mused. For a long moment she stared at him in pure feminine appreciation of his virile male form, the fast-becoming familiar feelings exploding inside her.

To get her mind off his sexy body, and under control, she asked, 'Where are we going? You never said.'

He flashed her a grin. 'All the way,' he drawled, and paused until he saw the colour flood her cheeks. 'Relax. To the New Forest, I hope.'

'You do know the way?' Beth queried.

'Don't worry, I have a picnic hamper in the back. We can eat in the car if we have to.'

But they did not have to. Dex soon parked along a forest trail at the edge of a clearing. Beth got out of the car and looked around in delight: a more perfect destination would be hard to find. The New Forest in October, with its deciduous trees a blaze of red, yellow and gold, in stark contrast to the deep dark green of the pines, was a feast for the eyes.

Roaming through the woods hand in hand, they spotted red squirrels, dozens of rabbits, and of course the wild ponies the forest was famous for, along with the unexpected pleasure of seeing a small deer. Returning to the car, Dex collected a hamper and blanket from the trunk. He spread the tartan rug on the ground beneath the branches of a massive oak tree and placed the hamper in the middle.

A hamper from the best department store in London, what else! Beth thought with a wry grin, but nothing could spoil her enjoyment of the afternoon and her companion. The unusual warmth of the autumn day saw them both shed their jackets and lounge on the blanket, the hamper between them. They investigated its contents and nibbled caviar and pâté, washed down with champagne. Then they dined on chicken and French bread, along with various cheeses, with fresh exotic fruits to finish. Finally, Beth collapsed flat on her back and fell asleep.

She stirred and turned her head; something was biting her ear, something else was crawling up her arm. Her eyes slowly opened. Not something but someone, she realised, with a leap of her heart.

'You look so irresistible when you sleep,' Dex's seductive voice rumbled in her ear.

Supporting himself on one elbow, his long body was hovering over her and his free hand was stroking gently up her arm while his mouth nuzzled her ear.

'Dex,' she murmured, 'where has the hamper gone?'

She had fallen asleep with the picnic basket acting as a barrier between them and had awakened to find herself almost joined with him from the hip down, the heat of his body burning through the fine fabric of her trousers.

'So practical and yet so perfect,' he opined softly, trailing a string of tiny kisses down from her ear to her mouth and gently back to the tip of her nose, his grey eyes smiling lazily down into hers.

Beth was totally captivated. She drank in the tangy masculine scent of his cologne, along with the exquisite frisson of excitement that tingled through her body as he moved his hard, muscular thigh restlessly against her, bringing a blush to her cheeks.

'I moved the damn thing because I thought you were never going to wake up, and I had a much more pressing appetite. I needed quite desperately to hold you, to kiss you.' And he did.

His mouth covered hers in a kiss of achingly tender passion, and Beth closed her eyes and gave herself up to the kaleidoscope of hitherto unknown sensations rioting within her.

'You drive me crazy, Beth.' He whispered the words against her throat, then, raising his head, he demanded huskily, 'Look at me, Beth. You will be mine?'

She opened her eyes, but his kiss had stolen her breath away and she could not speak. Instead, her body now shaken with unfamiliar feeling, she stared up at him, unconscious of the fact that her huge green eyes, under their thick lashes, and the soft, swollen fullness of her mouth combined with her aura of innocence were tantalising challenges to a man like Dex.

He smiled a soft, slow predatory grin. 'No answer, my sweet? Then let me persuade you.'

Shockingly, she knew she wanted him too. Heat

surged from the centre of her body to every part of her as she recognized the power he had over her.

'But—' They were lying on a blanket in broad daylight; anyone could walk past, she meant to say. The words caught in her throat as his hand slid slowly across her breast and his head descended. His tongue flicked teasingly around her mouth, enticing a response she was helpless to withhold—did not want to!

With devastating intent, Dex carried on kissing her, parting her swollen lips, his tongue delving deep, and any lingering inhibitions Beth might have felt were vanquished by his sexual expertise. She ardently returned his kisses, her small hand curving around his neck to hold his head down to hers.

'At last,' he growled against her parted lips, 'you want me.' And, lifting his head, his silver eyes staring down into hers, he added, 'And God knows I want you. I ache.'

Beth lay immobile, trapped by the long leg he had moved over hers, the hard, masculine length of him making her vitally aware of exactly how much he wanted her, while her pulse-rate shot off the Richter scale. She made no objection when, with a deftness that underlined his vast experience, his long fingers unbuttoned her blouse. But when he deliberately drew back she could not hold back the soft sigh of regret that escaped her.

'Ah, shame,' he teased her, 'today you're wearing a bra.' In a second the front fastening was flicked open and he had peeled back both shirt and bra. 'If that was meant to deter me, Beth, it didn't work,' he mocked softly, his glittering gaze studying her naked breasts with lazy pleasure. 'You are so beautiful, and so perfect.'

Beth felt her whole body blush, the blood rushing through her veins like quicksilver. Her green eyes roamed, helpless with longing, over his handsome face—noting the darkening flush across his high cheek-bones, the sensuous twist to his full lips, and she shivered in anticipation as his dark head lowered slowly, not to her mouth, but to the rosy tip of her breast.

She had never allowed any other man such intimacy, but she was helpless where Dex was concerned. What she had feared was true: she could not deny him anything. Her hands tangled in the black silk curls of his head while her slender body arched involuntarily towards the source of its pleasure. He slowly sucked her taut nipple into his mouth, rolling his tongue around the rigid peak until she moaned out loud. When he moved to give the same treatment to her other breast, she thought she would faint with the pleasure.

She made no demur when his hard-muscled thigh gently nudged her trembling legs apart, or when he swiftly unzipped her trousers and eased one large hand down over her flat stomach. She felt an instant of loss when his mouth deserted her breast and he reared up. But his passion-darkened eyes, glittering with a ferocious need, told her he was not deserting her, and then, once more, his mouth sought hers in a possessive, hungry kiss.

Beth traced his broad shoulders with trembling hands, moving them down to slide them up beneath his sweater. The feel of his satin flesh was an aphrodisiac all on its own. She felt his great body shudder, and gloried in his hard-muscled flesh. Moist heat flooded her loins as a teasing finger eased beneath her scanty briefs and found the secret part of her. It was only when he rolled over her, covering her completely, and she could feel the rigid length of his masculine arousal hard against her, that she panicked like the frightened virgin she was.

Her eyes flew wide open. She saw the swaying branches of the tree and the blue sky above. What was she inviting? 'No! No, Dex.' She squirmed beneath him, her small hand closing over his strong wrist. 'I can't!' Though every nerve in her body was crying out with need, her fear of the unknown, ultimate intimacy was greater, and she began to struggle in earnest.

'No? You can't say no—not now, Beth.' His throaty voice grated on her taut nerves, his fingers flexing as though to throw off her hold on his wrist.

'Please stop.' For a long moment she thought Dex was going to ignore her plea. His full weight pinned her down and he buried his head in the blanket over her shoulder. She felt his long body shudder and heard him groan, and then suddenly he rolled off her to lie on his back.

'I'm sorry,' she whispered, her body still pulsing with aching desire. Though she wasn't exactly sure what she was apologising for.

'Not half as sorry as I am,' he snarled, jumping to his feet to tower over her. 'I despise women who play games.'

She gazed up at him in disbelief. The lover of a moment ago was gone, replaced by a furiously angry man. His grey eyes narrowed contemptuously on her half-naked, dishevelled form. 'Get dressed, before I forget I am a gentleman and take what you are so obviously begging for but haven't the guts to admit.'

The contempt in his tone, the ice in his eyes, cut her to the heart. She lowered her own eyes and was forcibly reminded of his aroused state, which he made no attempt to hide. Bending her head, she hastily fastened her clothes. He was right; she did want him. But not like this, under a tree in the open where all could see, with no commitment on his part other than a desire for sex.

With that thought uppermost in her mind, some of Beth's pride and common sense surfaced. It was not all her fault. Dex was just as guilty as she was; after all, it was Dex who had started making love to her, not the other way around. The frustration seething in her over-heated body, and a strong sense of pique at his attitude, gave her the determination to get to her feet, and, tilting her head back, she looked him straight in the eye.

'If you were a gentleman you would not have tried to seduce me in a public place anyway,' she said flatly.

'If—if...' he repeated furiously. 'God knows, I should have learnt my lesson by now. You are just like my—' He stopped, and as she watched a subtle change came over his features. 'Forget it. I have,' Dex finished tightly, and, swinging on his heel, he snatched up the hamper that had been cast to one side and headed for the car.

But Beth was intrigued, as well as stubborn. 'You can't just walk away, Dex.' But she was talking to his back. Hurrying after him, she caught his arm. 'Who am I like?' she demanded.

Dex turned, brushing her hand from his arm, and he stared at down at her. For a long moment the silence stretched between them, and Beth thought he was not going to answer. Then, suddenly, he spoke.

'You are totally unique, Beth, and I am a frustrated jerk. And I should have had more sense than to make love out in the open like a callow youth.' He smiled with a twist of his firm lips. 'You would probably prefer an older man with more restraint than I possess, I think.'

She should have been satisfied. His earlier anger had gone and he was actually smiling at her. But the smile did not reach his eyes, and why the cynical crack about an older man? For a fleeting moment Beth recalled the episode in the casino, and wondered again if he was jealous of Paul. No, Dex couldn't be; maybe it was just his possessive Latin nature. Or maybe, she realised suddenly, he was simply trying to change the subject. He hadn't answered her question, and Beth could not let it go.

'And I think you're avoiding my question. You said I was just like someone. Who?'

'Tenacious little thing, aren't you?' Moving closer, he linked his hands loosely around Beth's back in a non-threatening embrace. 'I was going to say my sister. You are exactly like her. Sweet, and certainly not the type to have sex with a man without some form of commitment, like a ring on your finger. I am right? No?' he queried.

His grey eyes caught and held Beth's, the intensity of his gaze leaving her in no doubt of his sincerity. He understood... She heaved a deep sigh of relief, a broad grin lighting up her lovely face.

'You know me so well,' she said, with a toss of her auburn curls.

'Not as well as I would like, though I have a very strong feeling that will be remedied eventually. But I promise not to rush you.'

But rush her he did, though surprisingly not in a sexual way. Which was why, five days later, Beth stood in front of the mirror in her bedroom eyeing her reflection and chewing nervously on her bottom lip. The exquisitely tailored cashmere coat in palest cream, was a perfect fit. Designed by a top Italian fashion house and purchased by Dex.

She had seen him every day since their picnic on Sunday. They had dined out every night. Dex had a talent for finding the most intimate little restaurants. They'd also driven out into the country and visited quaint pubs. They'd talked about their likes and dislikes. Beth loved Elton John and opera, and Dex—a typical Italian—loved opera too, knew every aria ever written by heart. But when he'd tried to sing, Beth had burst into fits of laughter. Surprisingly, he was totally tone deaf.

When Beth had tried to explain that, as a working girl, she needed to stay home some nights, he had overruled her objections, but had been considerate enough to make sure she was home by about eleven. They usually parted on the doorstep with a chaste goodnight kiss. In fact, Dex had behaved as a perfect gentleman: no sexual advances. But in every other respect he always got his own way, Beth ruefully admitted to herself.

The coat was a case in point. Dex had insisted on buying it for her when they had met for lunch the day before. At first he had wanted to buy her a mink coat, and when she had flatly refused he had compromised with the cashmere, overriding all her objections, by finally saying, 'You're a beautiful woman and you deserve beautiful clothes. I love England, but not even the English like the climate. You are my woman and I have no intention of letting you catch cold.'

His high-handed attitude rankled, but his 'my woman' had secretly thrilled her. So she had accepted the coat.

Later that evening, clinging to Dex's arm as they walked along the riverside towards the boat where they were to dine, she was glad of its warmth. But, once seated at a table for two, with the banks of the Thames passing by, the millions of city lights reflected in the dark waters, she had no need of its warmth. The romantic setting, the heat of Dex's gaze, his hand holding hers, the latent desire in his eyes lit a flame inside her that she knew would burn for ever.

It was over coffee that Dex dropped his bombshell.

'Have I told you tonight how lovely you are?' Reaching for her hand, he turned it over in his own, his thumb idly stroking the palm.

There was nothing idle about Beth's reaction; she could feel a tingling sensation right down to her toes. 'Yes, a dozen times,' she responded huskily, her starry eyes roaming over his chiselled features. He was so attractive, sometimes she had to pinch herself to make sure what was happening was real and not a fairy tale. She had seen the avid glances the other female diners cast in his direction. He was certainly the most dynamic virile man in this floating palace of a restaurant.

'You have that effect on me, Beth. I'm so besotted by you, I end up repeating myself like a parrot.'

'You! A parrot! Never,' she exclaimed. 'A hawk, now... That I could believe,' she teased, while hugging his words to her heart.

'Parrot, hawk—whatever. But this bird has to fly away tomorrow.'

'You're leaving?' Beth could not hide her consternation. 'But when? Why?'

'As it happens, I have promised my sister I will attend her birthday party in Italy tomorrow night. But, that aside, I have to be in New York on Monday. I do have a business to run, Beth. Usually I only visit London once or twice a year at most. Surely you must have realised I cannot stay here indefinitely.'

The more he talked, the more her heart sank. So much for her fairy tale romance. Dex was leaving. Withdrawing her hand from his, she picked up her coffee cup and drained it, then replacing it carefully on the table, she looked back at him.

'Yes, of course. I mean, who would want to spend their life living in one of the best hotels in London?' She tried to joke but her voice shook, and it took an almighty effort of will simply to hold his gaze. But Dex saw through her charade immediately.

'It is not the end of our relationship, Beth. In fact, it could be the beginning.' Grasping her hand once more, his eyes narrowed intently on her face. 'You can meet me in New York. I will arrange it, and I promise you will have a great time.'

Beth's heart lurched in her breast. The desire flaring in his eyes was a potent reminder of how it could be between them. If she let it... But common sense prevailed. How could she take off around the world with Dex? Just like that? There was her work, her friends, her apartment. And what exactly was Dex offering? She noted he had not asked her to his sister's birthday party; he was not about to introduce her to his family.

Obviously a brief fling at best was all he had in mind.

'No, sorry. I have to be at work on Monday,' she managed to say prosaically.

'Of course, foolish of me to ask.' Dropping her hand, he signalled for the waiter and ordered a brandy.

The boat docked some five minutes later; the diners were allowed to linger, but Dex suddenly seemed in a hurry to leave. He paid the bill, and, slipping the coat he had given her over her shoulders, urged her back on shore. The walk to the car and the drive back to her apartment were completed in silence.

Beth cast a few sidelong glances at her companion, but he appeared deep in thought and disturbingly remote. Had she blown her chances by refusing to go away with him? The thought hurt, but her sensible side told her it would hurt a whole lot more if she gave in to his demands and had a brief, lustful affair.

Finally, when Dex stopped the car outside her apartment, he turned in his seat and spoke. 'Would a ring make a difference, Beth?'

She shot him a startled glance, not sure she had heard correctly. 'A ring?' she queried. His features were shadowed in the dim light and she could not read his expression. But his husky chuckle was all too audible.

'Why the surprise, Beth? After last Sunday, I should have realised it is the obvious solution. I want you in my bed and in my life.'

God alone knew that was where Beth wanted to be, but she couldn't hide her amazement. Wide-eyed, she stared at Dex. Was he actually proposing?

'You mean an engagement ring?' She couldn't believe her ears.

'Of course. And, sliding his hand into the inside pocket of his jacket, he produced a small velvet ring box. 'I hope you like it, Beth, darling.'

She stared transfixed at the diamond solitaire ring nestling in the open box. 'You mean it? You really mean it?' It was all her wildest dreams come true. She turned moist luminous green eyes up to Dex, emotion overcoming her.

'You love me, you want to marry me,' she said, in a voice that shook with the enormity of the occasion.

'Of course.' And, lifting her left hand to his lips, he sucked gently on the third finger of her hand.

His lips felt like a ring of fire, and a million sensations flooded through Beth's slender frame.

Dex's silver eyes smiled into hers, and gently he slipped the diamond ring onto her wet finger. Then, folding her fingers in his huge hand, he murmured huskily, 'Consider yourself engaged, hmm?'

'Engaged?' Beth repeated.

'Heaven forbid. You have caught my parrot syndrome.' Dex chuckled again, a dark melodious sound, and with consummate ease slid her into his arms, kissing her with a thoroughness that left her a long time later staring bemused and breathless up into his darkly handsome face.

'Now that is settled, do I finally get to see your bedroom?' he demanded throatily. 'Say yes. You know you want to.'

'But it's so sudden, and I still can't go to New York,' Beth mumbled stupidly, so bowled over by the ring, his proposal, his kisses—simply by the man. She couldn't think clearly. 'I have to be at work on Monday.'

His eyes narrowed, moving slowly over her, and his mouth twisted. 'You're right, as usual,' he agreed. 'I did promise not to rush you.'

She shook her head 'Oh, no, Dex.' She lifted her hand to his face, her finger tracing the firm line of his mouth. 'I didn't mean...'

'Hush, Beth, you're tired and I am an insensitive fool.' And, opening the car door, Dex slid out, came around to the passenger's side and helped Beth out. He picked her up and carried her in his arms into her apartment building. He set her on her feet at the door of her apartment and kissed her once more, before taking the key from her purse and opening it.

With a large hand on her back, he urged her inside. 'The bedroom can wait, but remember you are mine. I will be back on Friday. Be good.' Then he was gone.

Beth was left standing looking at the closed door, her head spinning and her heart pounding. She was engaged.

Dex loved her. They were going to be married. She stumbled across the room and sank down on the only armchair. She twisted the ring around on her finger, watching the dancing lights in the heart of the diamond, studying it from every angle. It was a token of his love and commitment. A soft sigh parted her love-swollen lips. She had foolishly let Dex leave, thinking she was still not ready to share the ultimate act of love, when in reality her whole being was crying out for his possession.

Later, as she climbed into her lonely bed, she licked her lips, savouring the taste of his kisses. Dex loved her, and on Friday she vowed she would show him just exactly how much she loved him...

CHAPTER FOUR

BETH yawned widely and snuggled deeper into the soft bed. Dex was right. She was tired. But a tiny disquieting thought hovered on the edge of her mind. For a newly engaged man Dex had shown marked restraint! Friday could not come quick enough, was her last thought before sleep claimed her.

She woke up the next morning to the ringing of the telephone.

'Sorry to wake you, Beth.' Dex's deep, sexy voice brought a dreamy smile to her sleep-flushed face.

'Any time,' she murmured.

'I'm at the airport and I couldn't leave without hearing the sound of your voice. How is my fiancée this morning?'

'Wishing you hadn't left last night,' Beth said boldly, his 'my fiancée' giving her the confidence to reveal her innermost thoughts.

'Now you tell me,' Dex groaned. 'And I'm leaving in a few minutes. Hold that thought until next weekend. *Ciao.*'

On Monday morning Beth glowed with happiness as she walked into the office. Everything looked different; she was an engaged lady, she thought, and, bubbling over with the joy of life and her marvellous love, she proudly displayed the diamond ring on her finger.

Within minutes, everyone in the firm knew; the female

employees oohed and ahhed over the ring, and asked a million questions, until Beth's head was buzzing.

Linking arms with her friend, Mary, she stepped out into the pale autumn sunshine and the two girls headed for the local delicatessen-cum-diner, where they usually ate lunch.

'Come on, Beth. Who exactly is he? What does he do? I want the whole story from the beginning.' Mary was a couple of years older than Beth, tall and slim, with cropped fair hair and blue eyes that saw far too much. 'Are you going to stay at work when you marry, and when is the wedding?'

The last question gave Beth pause for thought. She had not heard from Dex since his brief call on Saturday morning. They had never discussed a wedding date, or her work, and suddenly she was prey to all sorts of doubts. When she thought about it, Dex's proposal in the car had not been particularly romantic. In fact, she could not remember his exact words, except, 'Of course'.

For some reason she did not understand herself, Beth answered all Mary's questions very circumspectly. She simply said his name was Dex, and that they had met through mutual friends. But she had fallen in love with him at first sight.

Mary was genuinely happy for her. 'All right, I'm convinced you love him. But marriage, Beth. Isn't it a bit quick? Whirlwind romances can be notoriously fragile.'

Beset by a host of conflicting emotions, by the time Beth got back home on Monday evening she was thoroughly despondent. After all, she hardly knew Dex. A few days was not a very long time in which to decide to spend one's life with a man, as Mary had reminded her as they'd left the office together.

But Dex's telephone call from America, half an hour after she got home, cured her blues in seconds. He was coming back early. His plane would arrive on Wednesday, at noon.

'That's marvellous news. I've missed you,' Beth said happily.

'Yes, well, I've missed you,' he returned flatly, without much enthusiasm. But as he continued Beth realised why.

Unfortunately, Dex explained, the purchase of the casino had not gone as smoothly as he had thought. The casino director, a married man in his fifties, had apparently been having an affair with his very clever young secretary, a devious young woman chasing after a much older man.

The thought crossed Beth's mind that Dex really had a thing about women who dated older men, but she didn't get a chance to speak as Dex continued.

Apparently, completely against company policy, the director had entrusted the girl with the combination of the safe. The secretary had not turned up today. When the director had made enquiries at her home he had discovered she had vanished at the weekend, and a great deal of money from the casino had gone with her. The police had been informed and the girl would not get away with it.

'I'm sorry you're having problems, Dex.' Beth finally managed to get a word in, and she was almost sorry for the thief. Dex would be an implacable enemy. Dismissing the thought, she added, 'But I'm glad you're coming back.'

'No, Beth, I'm sorry for boring you with business, but

don't worry, I'll have everything sorted out within a few hours of arriving in England.' His voice deepening throatily, he added, 'I'll call at your apartment no later than four. Be ready and waiting; we'll have an early dinner, and a long, long night together, hmm?'

Beth was glad he couldn't see her blush, but, at her mumbled assent, his sexy chuckle told her he knew exactly how she was feeling.

She looked around the small living room for the umpteenth time; not a thing was out of place. She had taken the day off work to prepare for Dex's arrival and the apartment was immaculate. The fridge was stocked with a selection of goodies, plus a bottle of champagne, she had washed and pampered her slim body with essential oils, her hair was styled in a mass of curls on the top of her head, and her make-up was as perfect as she could make it. There was nothing more to do but wait.

Glancing at her wristwatch, she sighed. It was no good; it was already five-thirty, and if she sat around her apartment another minute she would go mad. Without giving herself time to question if her action was advisable, Beth grabbed her purse, slipped on a tailored red wool jacket, the companion to her short straight skirt, cast one last look around her immaculate home and walked out of the door.

Signalling a cab, she climbed into the back and gave the address of the Seymour Club. She could hang about no longer. Dex had told her to wait for him but he obviously hadn't expected to be so long at the club, so why not give him a surprise and meet him there…?

She walked into the foyer and headed for the gaming rooms, then Mr Black appeared.

'You are a member, madam?' Not a flicker of rec-
ognition crossed his swarthy face.

Not an auspicious start, Beth thought, and for a moment she was hit by a sudden attack of nerves. She hesitated, then, remembering she was the fiancée of the
owner, she said boldly, 'Mr Giordanni is expecting me,
I am his fiancée.' Waving her engagement ring in front
of his face, she added, 'If you remember, we met last
week.' She was relieved to see the glimmer of a smile
in the man's hard face.

'But, of course, Bethany Lawrence. Forgive me. Mr
Giordanni is in the office. You know the way.'

'Thank you,' Beth said with a broad grin. Dex was
here and in moments she would see him.

She pushed open the door of the outer office and
walked in. Standing by the desk was a rather flustered-
looking middle-aged woman, talking to someone on the
telephone.

'I'm sorry, sir, but as a temporary worker I don't do
overtime. I finish at six and I'm leaving now.'

As Beth watched, the woman's face turned scarlet.

'Don't worry, I won't be!' the woman yelled, and
slammed down the phone. Catching sight of Beth, she
said angrily, 'If you have come to see Mr Giordanni,
he's in there.' She indicated the door with a wildly waving hand. 'With some other chauvinist pig like himself
from America. Please yourself if you want to wait, but
I'm out of here and I won't be back. The man is a ty-
rant.' Picking up her purse, she pressed a button on the
telephone communication console and left.

Another bad omen, Beth thought glumly, as the other
woman slammed the door behind her. So, now what?
She eyed the closed door of the inner sanctum, and some

of her courage deserted her. Dex was in, but apparently he had company. Should she just barge in, or wait?

She walked to the desk and sat down in the functional swivel seat. Perhaps if she rang through and told Dex she was here... She eyed the machine in front of her, not quite sure how the thing worked, then tentatively picked up the receiver and pressed a button. To her horror a voice spoke—not over the telephone, but from the intercom...

'As you've terrified the secretary into leaving, there's nothing more to do here. These notes will have to wait until the morning. So how about you and I have a night on the town.'

Beth, not recognising the voice, replaced the telephone receiver, but the speaker continued.

'Remember those two models last time? I have Deirdre's phone number. What do you say?'

Beth stared aghast at the buttons in front of her. Which one switched the damn thing off? She didn't like the way the conversation was going, and she wished she didn't have to listen to it.

'Sorry, Bob, but unfortunately I have a prior engagement.'

At the sound of Dex's voice Beth's heart jumped, though his 'unfortunately' was not what she wanted to hear. But what followed was even worse.

'Some other time, maybe. But we can have a drink together before I leave. This particular girl won't mind waiting.'

Beth's hand fell from the machine. She no longer had any wish to switch the thing off. There was something about Dexter's tone of voice, his confident assumption that she would wait for him when, by her reckoning, he was already two hours late, that made her back stiffen

with outraged pride. It might be true, but he didn't have
to tell his friend.

'Easy, is she?'

'Surprisingly, no. Beth is amazingly resistant to my
charms, and clever with it,' Dexter said with a wry
laugh. 'Which is one of the reasons I got engaged to her
last week.'

The 'clever' part she didn't like. But Dex was de-
fending her, and now he would tell his friend the other
reason for their engagement was that he loved her, Beth
thought, relaxing slightly. But she could not have been
more wrong...

'My God, I don't believe it; one of the world's best-
known misogynists and you're engaged to be married.
Did you actually buy the woman a ring?'

'Yes, yes, I did.'

Dex sounded oddly defensive to Beth's ears, but at
least he had confirmed they were engaged. The bark of
laughter from the other man did nothing to reassure her.

'But I thought after the games your ex-wife, Caroline,
played on you, the money she grabbed, you vowed never
to marry again.'

Ex-wife... The words rang in Beth's head. Dex had
never once mentioned he had been married before. Her
lovely face went pale, and she pushed the chair back—
she really must make her presence known. Eaves-
dropping on a private conversation was despicable, and
it was not like her at all—even if it had been an accident.
But she froze at Dex's next words.

'Who said anything about marriage? It might never
come to that. Suffice it to say, the girl was going out
with Paul Morris and I saw a chance to put a stop to
that, and took it.'

'Ah, now I see. Your sister Anna is still nuts about Morris, is she?'

'Yes. Personally I can't fathom what she sees in the man, but she wants him, and you know me—I'll do anything to make sure Anna gets what she wants. Apparently, after a year together, Morris decided he was too old for Anna and told her she deserved someone younger, someone who could give her the family she craves... Which is ironic under the circumstances. But, anyway, they had an almighty row and he left Italy and returned to England.

'When I came over here on business last month, Anna came with me. She was determined to make it up with Morris. Unbeknown to me, she called his apartment and found out from his housekeeper where he was dining one night. Of course Anna persuaded me to take her out to dinner at the same restaurant. I never did get to eat that night. As soon as we arrived, Anna espied Morris with another woman, a younger woman than her. Knowing Anna's temper, you can guess what happened next. My first thought was to go after Morris, but Anna made me promise I wouldn't interfere, not so much as speak to the man.'

Beth's stomach churned. She felt sick; she had to get out. But she could not make herself move; the masculine-voiced conversation held her in masochistic fascination.

'So, how did you meet the girl if she was with Morris?' Bob asked.

'Pure coincidence—fate, if you like. You know Brice—we've done business with him before—he's after a new contract. A week or so after the restaurant fiasco, I had a meeting with him the same day his firm was throwing a party. A young couple arrived and did an impromptu dance—not very well, I might add—and the girl ended up flat on the floor.'

Beth heard the chuckles and the clink of glasses. They were drinking and laughing at her. What more evidence did she need of her own stupidity?

'At first I thought, Idiots! But when the girl gazed up at me, with great big green soulful eyes, I recognised her as Morris's dinner date. Beth is not the type I usually go for. She's young, and quite small, but there's something about her. I could see why Morris fancied her. And it gave me the perfect opportunity to help Anna without breaking my promise to her. The rest, as they say, is history. I decided to take her from Morris and give Anna a chance to get him back. It wasn't difficult; I let her know I was disgustingly rich, and, like all women, she was hooked.'

'But why on earth would you consider another gold-digger after Caroline? And, more importantly, why get engaged to the girl if you have no intention of marrying her?'

'I never actually said that, Bob. After all, I'm not getting any younger, and I would like a son and heir. I think Beth is young enough, and eager enough, to become quite an obedient wife.'

Beth had heard enough. More than enough. She stood up and swayed slightly. She put her hand down on the communication console to steady herself and ironically succeeded in doing what she should have done in the beginning: the voices stopped.

She closed her eyes, fighting back the tears. So, she was 'young enough, and eager enough, to be an obedient wife'. Now she knew what Dex really thought of her. A travesty of a smile contorted her lovely face. And it certainly had nothing to do with love! He had taken her out to stop her dating Paul Morris. But why? Why lie? Why go to such an extent for his sister?

She glanced down at her hand, still on the console. The diamond ring on her finger winked back. A token of love and commitment, she had thought; straightening, she wrenched the ring off her finger and stuffed it in her purse—she couldn't bear to look at it.

She needed to think, but not here, not now. Later she would feel the pain, the heartache, but her first priority was to get away without meeting Dex.

Silently she walked across the room, and, grasping the door handle, she hesitated and looked around the office. Streamlined, high-tech functional—a suitably sterile environment in which to lose one's dreams, her artistic mind thought bitterly. Opening the door, she left.

She ran down the stairs, oblivious to the casino's customers and out on to the street without being challenged. When she finally stopped running she collapsed against the railings of a smart townhouse, and with her arms wrapped around her waist she doubled over in pain.

'Are you all right, miss?' A voice broke into her anguished thoughts, and she looked up into the concerned face of a policeman.

'Yes, yes, I'm fine.' She forced herself to straighten up, and glanced around. A bus stop caught her eye.

'Are you sure?'

'Just out of breath. I was running for a bus,' she lied. But the policeman seemed to accept her statement.

Which was why, five minutes later, she was actually seated on a bus, staring vacantly out of the window as it chugged very slowly through the rush hour traffic. She had no idea where it was going and didn't care; she had simply shown the bus pass she used for work to the conductor and he had accepted it.

Wearily she laid her head against the window, the enormity of what had happened finally hitting her. Her so-called fiancé, the man of her dreams, didn't even like her, let alone love her. With her new-found knowledge of his real reason for taking her out, suddenly a lot of little things Dex had said and done made sense.

On their first date he had insisted on telling her how wealthy he was, something she had found uncomfortable. Now she knew why: he considered her, and apparently every other woman in the world, a gold-digger. Their first passionate kiss at the casino had simply been Dex's reaction to her talking to Paul Morris. Dex had been staking his claim, nothing more. His cynical comments about young women with old men suddenly made perfect sense. They had all been directed at Beth personally; it was how Dex actually saw her. She recalled the picnic, when he had said she was just like…and had stopped; he hadn't been comparing her to his sister, but to his ex-wife and the games she'd played.

He obviously considered his precious sister perfect. He would do anything for the woman—even get engaged to a girl he cared nothing about if he thought it would help his sister get her man.

Engaged. That was a laugh! The cost of a ring was nothing to a man of Dex's wealth. Mary had been right to warn Beth. Dex really was a bastard in every sense of the word. And Beth, fool that she was, had spent all day anticipating falling into his arms and into his bed tonight.

The tragedy of it all, Beth thought with a bone-deep anguish, was that it had all been so unnecessary. If Dex had just once been honest, had asked her a simple question, she would not now be sitting on a bus with a black void where her heart used to be… She could see it all so clearly now, could pinpoint the exact two days, when the farce that had led her to this point had begun. Gazing with sightless eyes at the darkness beyond the bus window, she relived the whole episode in her mind...

Beth looked around her with delight, then sent a beaming smile to her dinner companion. 'Paul, this is fabulous! I can't thank you enough.' Her green eyes sparkled in the small oval of her lovely face. 'Dining on Park Lane makes me feel quite deliciously decadent.'

'Unlike your mother, Beth, you couldn't be decadent if you tried.' Her strikingly handsome silver-haired companion responded with an indulgent smile.

He was so right, Beth mused. Her mother had married for the fifth time the year Beth turned eighteen. Beth hadn't seen her since, but she didn't care. She had long since given up any hope of a mother-daughter relationship.

But Paul Morris had been the one constant adult throughout her twenty-one years. He had been a friend of her father, and was her godfather. He had managed the small trust fund her father had settled on her for her education, and had supported her ambition to become a graphic artist, encouraging her to go to the local college in Torquay.

She'd quickly discovered, after graduating last July, that the scope for a budding graphic artist in her home county of Devon was limited. But Paul had stepped in and used his not inconsiderable clout to find her a job in the London advertising firm his own company used. He'd also helped her find a small apartment to rent in Docklands. She had been in London for over two months, and was so far loving every minute of it—and dining at one of the poshest restaurants in the city certainly helped!

Grinning back, she dismissed her musing and said jokingly, 'Oh, I don't know.' Eyeing the plate of exquisitely arranged noisettes of lamb, with accompanying vegetables, that the waiter was placing in front of her, she continued, 'I think I could very easily get used to this lifestyle.'

Paul raised his glass and Beth reciprocated. 'To you, Beth, and your future success as the greatest graphic artist ever. I might have pulled a few strings to get you in to Canary Characters, but according to Cecil, the art director, you're a natural—and nice with it. Which I always knew, anyway," he said with great satisfaction.

He was the father she had never really known, and probably the kindest person she had ever met. Emotion clogged her throat but, swallowing hard, she replied, 'To you, Paul; your help and understanding over the years have made me what I am today.'

They both sipped their champagne, a look of pure love and understanding passing between them. Then, all hell broke loose...

Out of the corner of her eye Beth saw a very attractive dark-haired woman approach the table. To her amazement, the woman picked up Paul's dinner plate and tipped his meal over his head.

'You bastard! You said *I* was too young...' With a vitriolic look in Beth's direction, the woman changed from English into a language that Beth recognised as Italian but which she did not understand—and that was maybe just as well, as she doubted the woman's words were complimentary.

Eyes like saucers, open-mouthed, Beth stared at Paul. Mint sauce was trickling down his forehead, a lamb noisette sat on his head, another on his shoulder, the rest of his food—small new potatoes and assorted vegetables—lay all over the table and in his lap. Stunned, she looked down at the glass still in her hand and eyed the single petit pois floating in it. Replacing the glass on the table, she carefully picked the tiny pea out of her champagne.

She had read books where the hero got spaghetti tipped over him by some irate woman, but somehow lamb and potatoes did not have the same effect, Beth thought inconsequentially, glancing back at Paul. He had risen to his feet and was saying something low and hard to the woman that obviously did not please her, if the fury in her dark eyes was anything to go by.

Suddenly a man appeared and encircled the lady's waist with a strong arm. He was tall, about six-two, and built like a barn door—or a double door, Beth amended in her mind. She couldn't see the man's face, only his very broad back, black hair and long, long legs, but it was enough to send a shiver of fear down her spine. She didn't fancy Paul's chances with this burly hunk, obviously bristling with male aggression.

But she need not have worried. In a matter of seconds the stranger was ushering the woman straight on, and out of the restaurant.

Her face reflecting her astonishment, Beth glanced up at Paul, and he, with the sophistication of the true gentleman, first asked Beth if she was all right and apologised for the interruption, then calmly instructed the *maître d'* to have the table reset and their order replaced.

Beth grabbed Paul's sleeve. 'Surely you don't want to stay here now?' she whispered urgently, suddenly aware of the amused looks of the rest of the diners, and blushing scarlet with embarrassment.

'Beth, darling,' he soothed, removing her hand from his sleeve and nonchalantly brushing himself down with his napkin before resuming his seat, 'remember the stiff upper lip and all that. The mark of a true Englishman is to remain cool, whatever the circumstances. Besides which, I'm hungry, and I have no intention of forgoing my meal for some over-excitable Latin female.'

'But who was she? And why did she—?'

Paul held up a hand. 'Forget her, Beth. I already have.'

'But she was furious…'

'I know—her type always are. I think it's one of nature's little tricks on the male of the species. While one prefers a fiery, passionate woman in bed, one avoids them like the plague out of it. Which is probably why I have never married.'

'You're incredible.' Beth grinned, with a rueful shake of her long auburn hair, the humour of the situation finally getting through to her. 'And you have sauce on your brow and cheek.'

Paul allowed the slightest trace of a smile to lighten his face before saying, 'Then will you excuse me a moment while I slip to the restroom?'

Of course Beth did, and when he returned, and their dinner was once again set before them, Beth said admiringly, 'You really are amazing, Paul. So suave. Most men would have died of embarrassment and rushed out of the restaurant after such an outrageous scene.'

'Put it down to years at prep school and Eton, and forget about it, Beth, darling. Enjoy your food before it gets cold.' Amazingly she did…

By the time Paul stopped his sleek black car outside the entrance to her apartment they were both in fits of laughter over the whole unfortunate episode. But later, curled up in bed, for an instant Beth wondered just exactly what kind of relationship Paul had with the unfortunate woman, and for a second felt a fleeting compassion for the lady.

Although Paul was like a father figure to her, she was woman enough to realise that he was a very attractive man. Tall, elegant and wealthy, he had inherited an estate in Devon and a vineyard in southern Italy from his parents, plus he didn't look his fifty-three years. In fact he was a very eligible bachelor, dividing his time between his two estates throughout the year, with frequent visits to his penthouse in London, behaving as a typical man about town. Perhaps he had been playing around with the woman... But, then again, she thought, just before sleep claimed her, the woman hadn't been alone at the restaurant. Beth had only seen the rear of her companion, but he had been quite a man...

At six o'clock the next afternoon, as Beth walked out of the elevator on the ground floor of the office block that housed Canary Characters, she looked up to see Paul walking in the door. They looked at each other and grinned.

'I won't mention last night if you don't,' Beth offered.

'That's what I love about you, Bethany Lawrence,' said Paul, giving her her full name. 'You have your mother's looks, but you definitely have your father's nature. Such a sensible girl. Now, how about coming out for an early dinner with me tonight? This time I can assure you it will be a totally uneventful evening.'

Of course she agreed, and after a quiet meal in a small bistro, Paul again drove her home.

Standing on the doorstep at the entrance to her apartment block, Beth turned to Paul. 'Would you like to come up for a coffee, or do you have a more pressing date?' she teased; it was only ten in the evening, and she knew his passion for the casinos when he was in town.

'For a young girl you are far too cynical and know me far too well.' Reaching out his hand, he stroked her cheek with the back of his knuckles. 'You're right, the tables await, and, as I intend spending the next few months stuck in the middle of the Italian countryside, I'd better be off. Look after yourself, and be good. You know how to get in touch if you need me.'

'Yes, and thank you again for everything, Paul.' Flinging her arms around him, she gave him a hug and pressed a soft kiss to his smooth cheek. 'And you be good as well.' Stepping back, she grinned. 'If you can, you old reprobate.' And with a last flashing smile she hurried inside.

Striding across the lobby with a spring in her step, Beth wondered when she would see Paul again. Sometimes there were months between their meetings, and, although she knew he was always there for her on the end of the telephone, she missed his company. But then he had his own life to lead, and she had hers. Her new job was going well; she had made friends with Mary, a new trainee like herself, and they often went for a meal or to the cinema, or simply gossiped over a drink. Life looked good... What more could a girl want?

Now Beth knew, and the knowledge caused her unimaginable pain. She had wanted Dex to love her, to marry her, but it had all been a game to him. Dex had taken her out to make sure she stayed away from Paul. That Dex actually thought she was the type of young girl who would date a man in his fifties simply because he was wealthy said it all. Dex had no respect for Beth as a person; he probably had no respect for any woman except his sister.

Thinking of Paul, and his comment about a stiff upper lip, she refused to cry, and swiftly brushed the tears from her eyes. Her full lips twisted in a bitter smile; coincidentally it was exactly three weeks tonight since her eventful dinner with Paul, and exactly thirteen days since she had fist met Dex. Unlucky thirteen was certainly true in her case...

'Hey, miss. Do you know where you're going?' The conductor's question broke into her bitter reverie.

'Sorry, where are we now?' she asked, stumbling to her feet.

'Corner of Leceister Square.'

'That's fine, thank you,' she murmured, brushing past him and stepping off the bus.

Beth looked around at the hordes of people, the flashing neon signs, and had never felt so alone in her life. She dearly wanted to cry, but she knew she couldn't. Not yet. She had nowhere to go except home, and if Dex wasn't waiting he would certainly call her. He was not the sort of man any woman stood up. She needed to have a plan, an excuse, some way to get rid of him without revealing what she knew. Pride alone would not let her behave any other way, and her pride was all she had left.

CHAPTER FIVE

STEPPING out of the tube station into the cool night air, Beth stiffened her shoulders and walked the short distance to her apartment building. She looked neither right nor left, her whole attention concentrated on the plan she had formed in her mind on the journey home. Her despair, after the destruction of all her hopes and dreams, had been replaced for the moment with an ice-cold fury.

No way was she going to tell Dex that Paul was her godfather; the swine and his sister could stew in hell for all she cared! They would find out eventually, no doubt, but certainly not from her.

'Where the hell have you been?' She was suddenly stopped in her tracks by a furiously angry Dex. His large hands grabbed her by the shoulders, and for a second she feared he was going to shake the life out of her. 'I have been sitting in the car for over four hours, waiting for you and being worried sick. Black told me you called at the club.'

She looked up into his darkly attractive face. The orange light of the street lamp cast flickering shadows over his chiselled features, and for an instant she actually thought she saw a shimmer of genuine worry in his steely eyes, but she was not fooled by it.

'Yes, I did, but what are you doing here? Didn't you get my note?' she managed to ask with a quizzical arch of one delicate brow, in an acting performance that would have done credit to a Hollywood movie star...

'Note? What note? What the hell are you talking about?'

he growled. 'And why am I having this conversation in the street?'

Beth was wondering the same; if she didn't sit down she would fall down, or worse, fall into his arms. His hands kneading her shoulders were playing havoc with her nerve-endings, and even though she knew he was a manipulative devil it didn't alter the fact that he was wickedly attractive.

'For God's sake, give me your key and let's get inside. This is not how I envisaged our reunion at all. I thought I told you to wait for me.'

His comment reminded her of his arrogant assumption to his friend—'This particular girl won't mind waiting'—and that was enough to stiffen her resolve.

'If you let go of me, I will,' she snapped. His hands fell from her shoulders, and she stepped back and silently withdrew the key from her purse and handed it to him.

He glanced down into her cool face. 'You look...' He stopped, his gaze piercingly intent. 'Never mind, it'll keep.' And he urged her inside the building and into her apartment without saying another word.

Beth could feel the tension simmering in the air between them, and when Dex's arm reached across her she shrank back, afraid he was going to grab her again.

Instead, with a sardonic arch of one dark brow, he drawled, 'Excuse me—unless you prefer the dark,' and switched on the light, slamming the door behind them.

Trying to behave naturally, when Beth's basic instinct was to turn on him like a howling banshee, took every ounce of self-control she possessed, but she succeeded. She walked into the centre of the room and, taking a deep breath, slowly turned to face him.

'Coffee, tea, something stronger?' she suggested, forcing a polite smile to her stiff lips. Dex was leaning against the closed door, his dark blue suit jacket hanging open, his tie pulled loose and the top few buttons of his silk shirt unbuttoned. He looked dishevelled and absolutely furious.

'I do not want a drink.' He straightened up and moved towards her, stopping only inches away. 'I want some answers, *cara*—my sweet fiancée.' He glared down at her and there was nothing in the least sweet about his expression.

'Well, I want a drink,' she said calmly, turning towards the kitchen door. 'Take a seat. I won't be long.'

'Oh, no, you don't!' A strong masculine hand encircled her upper arm, and suddenly she was spun back round to face him.

Her green eyes clashed with his, and something sinister flickered in the depths of his grey eyes that made her shiver with alarm. 'Please, let go of me,' she told him, trying to ignore the way her heart was thudding as he stood so close to her.

'I would never intentionally hurt you, Beth,' Dex declared silkily, and with slow deliberation he released her arm and slid his hands up to her shoulders, impelling her forward. 'Never,' he reiterated throatily.

His black head bent towards her and dumbly she watched, knowing he was going to kiss her, and unable to move. Then his mouth took hers in a forceful, demanding kiss. Beth clenched her teeth against his intended invasion. A silent moan of rejection rose and died in her throat beneath the relentless pressure of his mouth. His hands slid down her back and effortlessly brought her even closer against his masculine frame. Try as she might to remain cold and unresponsive in his arms, there was nothing she could do to prevent her wayward body melting against his hard length.

A soundless gasp escaped her lips, and, taking full advantage, his tongue sought the moist interior of her mouth with a coaxing, seductive sensuality that made her mind spin. Her eyes closed as he easily overcame her futile attempt to resist, and helplessly she kissed him back.

When Dex finally released her, she swayed and almost fell, but with a husky oath he curved a long arm around her waist and firm fingers lifted her chin.

'I should have kissed you first,' he opined, with a hint of arrogance in his smile, 'instead of shouting at you. I am sure you have a simple explanation. Forgive me.'

His grey-eyed gaze had changed from menacing anger to smug complacency at her submission, Beth noted bitterly. Forgive him! She wanted to kill him, and, swiftly lowering her lashes to hide the anger and humiliation she knew he would see in their depths, she began her well-rehearsed speech.

'No, Dex, it is you who has to forgive me.' Turning her head to dislodge his fingers, she twisted out of his arm, not at all sure her trembling legs would support her. She sat down in the one comfortable chair, her head bowed, her hands curled tensely over its arms, and added, 'I left a note with your secretary at the casino, telling you I had to visit a sick friend in hospital.'

Beth had thought it out carefully. Judging by the temporary secretary's outburst in Beth's hearing, it was highly unlikely the woman would ever return to work at the Seymour, so Beth felt reasonably safe with the lie. The timing was wrong, she had left long after the secretary, but no one had seen her leave, and she was bank-

ing on the great Dexter Giordanni not bothering to en-
quire. Why should he? He didn't give a damn about her.

For a long moment there was silence, and Beth could
sense the force of his gaze upon her downbent head. It
took all her self-control to lift her head and look at him.

'I didn't receive a note, but then I didn't see the secretary leave,' he said, his puzzled gaze holding hers.

'There you are, then…a simple mistake. Let's forget
it.' And in an abrupt change of subject she went on, 'So
tell me, did your sister have a nice birthday party? You
never said.' Beth couldn't resist asking, hoping just once
to dent his insufferable self-assurance. Cynically she
watched as his grey gaze roamed over her and rested
where her hands lay curled on the edges of the armchair.

'Yes, I don't see her very often, so it was a nice
change.' He frowned and continued, 'A pity you could
not come with me.'

Liar, she thought scathingly. He had never asked her.
Probably too worried that Paul Morris would be there,
and Beth would spoil his sister's chance with the man.
His careful avoidance of her gaze only reaffirmed what
she already knew.

But suddenly his head jerked back and his eyes narrowed intently on her face, a flash of some unidentifiable
emotion flickering in their icy depths; then they became
hard and implacable, his massive body unnaturally still.

'Forget the small-talk, Beth. You haven't visited any
sick friend; you're lying, and I want the truth,' he
warned inflexibly. 'And it had better be good. I am not
known for my patience, and you are testing it to the
limit.'

The temptation to tell him precisely what he could do
with himself and his patience was almost impossible to

ignore. But pride and common sense raised their logical heads just in time.

'Yes, I did. Mary from work,' she responded flatly, lying through her teeth and praying Mary would forgive her. 'Appendicitis,' she tacked on for good measure.

'Really?' Dex drawled, his tone telling her he didn't believe a word she said. 'Nice outfit. Chanel, isn't it? It suits you. Your friend must have been flattered.'

'Yes,' Beth said shortly, cursing her own foolishness yesterday, which had seen her spending her lunchbreak shopping in the designer section of London's most stylish fashion store. She had spent all her savings, and her next month's salary, on the elegant red suit and complementary camisole, plus ruinously expensive undergarments, all for Dexter's benefit.

'Surely a bit over the top for visiting a sick friend,' Dex commented derisively. 'Nor, to my knowledge, do hospitals extend their visiting hours until this time of night. What kind of fool do you take me for?'

She glanced up. His tanned, perfectly carved features were set in a cold mask, only the nerve twitching in the side of his face revealing his inner tension.

'I don't know what you mean,' she mumbled. Her courage had deserted her, and she couldn't control the nervous leaping of her pulse, or the shiver of fear that trickled down her spine as her eyes met his.

Suddenly, like a dam bursting, *'Basta!'* Dex roared. 'Enough of your lies!' His hands crashed down on her shoulders, the long fingers biting into her skin as he hauled her to her feet, fury evident in every line of his hard body.

'Now,' he snarled, 'you are going to tell me the truth.' His long fingers fell to her jacket and flicked it open, revealing the lace edged body-hugging camisole and the obvious absence of a bra.

She flushed scarlet. 'What do you think you're doing?' she snapped, but Dex ignored her, and in one lithe movement he slipped the jacket from her shoulders to drop it carelessly on the floor.

His glittering eyes raked over her, from her flushed face, then lower, to the soft fullness of her breasts. To her horror, she felt her nipples harden beneath his studied appraisal. With chilling slowness his glance lingered on her chest, her throat, and finally back on her face. He smiled and her blood ran cold.

'Very nice, but you are not the type to dress so for another woman.' His hand snaked around her slender wrist and hauled her hand up between their two bodies, holding it pressed tight against her breastbone.

'And I seem to remember giving you a diamond ring, *cara mia*. Lost it, have you?' His mouth twisted in a chilling, cynical smile. 'Or found someone wealthier? Someone who excites you more?'

Beth swallowed hard, remembering some of their more intimate moments together, and glanced bitterly up at him. Surely he knew? He was the only man who had ever aroused her to any great degree. How dared he insinuate she was a money-grubbing, flighty girl—she who had never known a man? For a moment Beth was too angry with him to form a reply. When she did open her mouth to speak, she discovered she had waited too long.

'Your silence is answer enough. Are you going to tell me who he is?' he demanded in a threatening voice. 'Or do I have to get it out of you?'

His other hand tightened imperceptibly in her hair, and she moved her head back and stared at him. But the fury in his eyes, she realised, was more bruised ego than any genuine concern for her. He had jumped to the conclusion there was another man, whom he probably thought was her godfather, so why not humour him? Grasping the chance Dex had given her, she boldly held his glittering gaze.

'All right, all right. I will tell you the truth.' She gritted her mouth tight with bitterness as she prepared to compound her lie. To make Dex walk away from her. It was what she wanted. But as Dex towered over her— the heat of his body, the subtle scent of him enveloping her—it was the hardest thing she had ever had to do in her life.

'You're right, in a way. I'm sorry, Dex. I didn't know how to tell you.' When it came down to it, she didn't dare mention Paul Morris. For all she knew, Dex might have seen him in Italy. Instead, she rattled on like a steam train.

'I realised almost as soon as you left: you're not really my type, we belong to two different worlds. I like living in London, I love my work and I like going out with my own circle of friends. Some more than others.' She forced herself to smile into his eyes, subtly implying there were other men in her life, without naming any names. 'You and I had a brief fling. It was fun, but now it's over.'

His face darkened. His mouth tightened into an angry line and a dull flush spread over his high cheekbones. His fingers tightened on her wrist and she lowered her thick lashes to hide her lying eyes from his narrowed, too intent gaze. Then suddenly she was released and fell back into the armchair, all the breath expelled from her lungs by the force of her fall. When she finally found the courage to raise her head and look at Dex again, she knew she had succeeded in her plan.

He had gone very pale. His silver eyes, burning with contemptuous fire, clashed with her wary green. He shook his dark head. 'You're just like all the rest, a lying, cheating, little bitch,' he drawled deliberately, watching her for a moment. Then, turning, he headed for the door.

How dared he call her names? How dared he pretend he was the one betrayed, when it was Beth who had been made a complete and utter fool of? He had even gone so far as to give her a ring. The ring! she thought, eyeing his broad back with impotent fury, and, grabbing her purse from the floor, she opened it. Her fingers finding the offending piece of jewellery, she stood up.

'Dex, wait!' He halted and turned. Beth stretched out her arm, 'Haven't you forgotten something?' she mocked with a cruel smile, giving him some of his own medicine. 'Your ring.'

Dex stood in the doorway, his features a hard mask of indifference. 'Keep it,' he said bitingly. 'A memento of a failed affair. Unless, of course, you want to pay for it in kind.' He smiled with a chilling twist of his hard mouth. 'Unlike the dozens before me, I still have not seen your bedroom.'

This mocking cynicism was the last straw for Beth's over-stretched nerves. Flinging the ring at him, she yelled, 'Get out. Go, go!' And the ring bounced off his cheek and fell to the floor.

His steel-grey eyes flashed with inimicable fury, and like a prowling panther he stalked back towards her. Beth knew she had gone too far. Her heart leapt in her throat as she backed warily away from him. A spot of blood stained his high cheekbone. Served him right, she told herself. Why should she have to put up with his contemptuous remarks, while Dex pretended his motives were pure as the driven snow?

'No one tells me to leave,' he stated softly, in a low tone.

'Until now,' she shot back, refusing to be intimidated but no longer feeling quite so brave as his advance had her backing closer into the hall that led to her bedroom.

'Never, ever,' he drawled quietly, and, catching her by the shoulders, he drew her close. 'And certainly not a devious little girl like you.'

Beth could not prevent the shiver that his large hands on her naked shoulder aroused, and he grinned, with a wolfish twist of his hard mouth.

'A little girl who doesn't know whether she wants to jilt me or jump me,' he mocked with biting sarcasm. 'I think we really need to know the answer, Bethany. Don't you?'

'No, no!' she cried, the implacable determination in his expression telling her exactly what he had in mind. She shuddered as his hands slid caressingly over her shoulders and closed firmly around her upper arms. She wanted to yell at him to stop, but the words stuck in her throat as, with slow deliberation, Dex lifted her up and buried his face in the valley between her breasts. He moved ever so slightly, his mouth covering the tip of her breast which was barely hidden from his view by the fine silk of the ridiculously brief camisole she was wearing.

She grasped his dark head to steady herself. 'Put me down,' she cried, her feet flailing wildly in mid-air, trying to kick him. But she was helpless against his superior height and strength, and, worse, against the exquisite sensations his warm mouth was creating as he continued to nuzzle her breasts.

'I will,' he said silkily, lowering her so they were face to face, 'as soon as I find the bedroom.'

'No!' she cried, disgusted at her own reaction.

But he carried her into the inner hall, deaf to her protest, and shouldered open the bedroom door.

'You can't do this. Put me down!'

'I can, and I will,' he grated, and suddenly Beth found herself sprawled on her back on her own bed, with all the breath knocked out of her. Stunned, she stared as, in a split second, Dex shed his jacket, tie and shrugged out of his shirt.

His muscular chest, tanned and with a light covering of black curling body hair, was a breathtaking sight. A dark line of hair arrowed tantalisingly down to his waist, where his long fingers snapped open the band of his trousers

Beth's green eyes widened to their fullest extent in a mixture of horror and fascination. Dear God, he was stripping! 'You can't do that!' He ignored her. 'Get out! I demand you leave!' He stepped out of his trousers. 'Put them on! Stop it!' she babbled, her voice shrill; he was naked except for a pair of white briefs that did little to hide his maleness. Swallowing hard, she scrambled to sit up. But she was too late.

'Oh, no!' Dex had joined her on the bed; what seemed like acres of naked chest leaned over her, and, raking his hand through her long hair, he lifted her head and his mouth covered hers.

Beth had expected harshness, but he confounded her with the soft pressure of his lips; his tongue traced the outline of her mouth while his other hand slid up over her breast and cupped its lush fullness. She groaned, and his tongue snatched the advantage to plunge between her parted lips.

It wasn't fair! she silently screamed, the echo fading n her mind as Dex continued to kiss her, his mouth exploring hers with sensual expertise. His hands began moving slowly over her breasts, slipping the thin straps of the camisole down over her slender shoulders. Her heartbeat quickened and she shook with the effort of trying to control the effect he was having.

His anger she could have resisted, but the caressing touch of his hands cupping her now naked breasts, and the feather-light brush of his fingers over the hardening peaks, sent sharp stabs of excitement shooting through her. Beth felt herself beginning to weaken. The reason for her fury with him seemed nothing in comparison to the sensual pleasure he was awakening in her.

He raised his head, his glittering eyes raking over her full breasts, their rigid nipples, and a slow, sensual smile curved his hard mouth as he deftly pushed the camisole and her skirt down over her slender hips.

'No,' she croaked, every nerve-ending in her body screaming with her effort to retain control of her drowning senses.

'Yes, Beth, yes. You want me. You know you do.' His dark head bent and his tongue licked teasingly over her breasts.

Beth groaned out loud and she arched against the hard heat of him as electric sensation spun from her breasts to her stomach. She grabbed his dark head and made a last futile attempt to push him away, then he drew one aching nipple into his mouth and she was lost. Instead of pushing him away, her fingers involuntarily tangled in the silky black hair of his head, caressing his scalp.

'That's it, Beth,' he rasped, moving slightly to give the same erotic concentration to her other breast. 'Let yourself go, sweetheart.'

Dex's strong, masculine hand traced the indentation
of her waist, down over her stomach and across her
thighs, taking her briefs with it. She shuddered as his
long fingers stroked across her inner thigh and tangled
in the dark red curls protecting the core of her feminin-
ity.

Beth's fingers clenched in his hair and then slowly
they unfurled. Her slender arms moved tentatively
around his broad back, her fingers tracing the line of his
spine. The brush of his chest hair against her sensitised
flesh was a sweet agony as his lips moved over her throat
and found her parted lips once again.

His mouth closed over hers, his tongue fierce and
seeking, and her response was immediate. Her body
writhed helplessly beneath him; her hands slid down his
back and curved around the tight male buttocks. When
had he removed his briefs? She didn't know, and was
past caring.

Dex nudged apart her legs and Beth shuddered, and
shuddered again as his lips ground against hers in a hungry, rapacious kiss, while his fingers found those other
secret lips and teased and tormented the delicate moist
flesh again and again.

Never had she known such delicious sensations. His
hard male body, the musky smell of sex, the tactile
delight she found in touching him, and the incredible
quivering in the pit of her belly. Still, a tiny lone voice
of sanity told her she must say no. But, God help her,
she didn't want to. Her body screamed out to know
where his delicious assault would lead.

Beth looked up into his silver eyes, only inches from
her own, and her heart stopped; the ferocious gleam of
unbridled passion—more a glint of scarcely controlled

age—got through her drugged senses for a second, and she tensed.

Sensing her brief withdrawal, Dex growled, 'No, Beth, not now,' and deliberately rolled over between her thighs. His powerful body trapped her beneath him and his strong hand clasped her shoulders, pinning her to the bed. He reared back, his glance skimming over the length of her, her lush, full breasts. Sliding his hands from her shoulders to her chest, he rolled the turgid peaks between his fingers and thumbs. Then his hands roamed on at will over her burning flesh, the hard rigid length of his manhood pushing against her groin but no further.

Beth looked into his face, her eyes clouded with passion. She saw his sensuous lips quirk in a wickedly determined smile as he slowly lowered himself down upon her, but still he did not claim her. Instead he kissed her love-swollen lips long and hard, his hands still caressing that very secret part of her. Beth's arms curved around his back, her nails sinking into his broad shoulders in mute appeal. She wanted him now, filling her, anything to assuage the red-hot fire that burned through every vein and nerve in her trembling body.

Dex raised his head. 'Whoever you saw earlier certainly did nothing for you,' he grated, masculine triumph edging his tone. Reaching out to the bedside table, he picked up the protection he had placed there. 'I wonder how many other men have seen you like this, with your luscious body begging for them.'

She wanted to say, no one. To tell him the truth. But one hand stroked up deliberately to the engorged tip of her breast, and once more his mouth descended to it. His teeth bit gently, and she jerked helplessly; she was drowning in a sea of sensual delight and only Dex could save her. His mouth once more sought hers, his tongue thrusting, but this time his mighty body picked up the rhythm. He broke the kiss and raised his head, his grey eyes almost black with desire, fixed on her wildly flushed face.

'What do you want, Beth?' He surged against her again, his hard arousal sliding through the soft curls and between her trembling thighs, but still not giving her what her body craved.

'Say it, Beth…' A hard sheen of sweat glistened on his tanned skin. 'Say, I want you, Dex.' All the while his glittering eyes seared into hers.

Green eyes wide with wonder and want, she stared up into his face. He had betrayed her, but she loved him so much; she ached for him. Surely she deserved this one night of love. Was it so wrong? Instinctivley, she knew she would never again want a man as she did Dex. Then his hand slid between their two bodies and he touched her intimately again, parting her legs further, sending shock waves crashing though her.

'Please. I want you,' she confessed in a whisper, allowing her instincts to take over. She closed her eyes, her small hand stroking down his shoulder and over his chest, her fingers catching a male nipple, hard like a pebble and buried in lush black curling hair.

'Damn it! My name, Beth. Say my name.' His voice was a deep growl of masculine frustration.

'Dex,' she groaned, and pressed tiny hot kisses on his chest, her small hand stroking down the silky line of body hair to his flat belly.

Dex caught her hands and pulled them away from him, and, curving his large hands around her bottom, he drove into her with a fierce, thrusting, primeval power.

She felt a knife-like pain and cried out, but his mouth

overed hers and swallowed her cry with a voracious
iss. Then, for a moment, he was still.

His molten silver eyes burned into hers and he spoke
n a torrent of Italian, not one word of which she un-
erstood. But the pain she had felt at his possession had
ubsided and her muscles tightened around him. This
vas no forced lovemaking. Dex was right; she had asked
im to take her. Then, slowly, he withdrew.

'No, please!' He could not stop now. She moaned,
nd suddenly she was clinging to him as he moved in
er once again, his huge body moving in a hard thrusting
hythm that sent her to the edge of some unknown cata-
lysmic state.

Then she was crying his name, and tipping over the
dge into free-fall, her whole body shattering into a mil-
ion atoms and, by some miracle, clenching over and
ver, and reforming again in a shattering climax. She
elt Dex's great body shudder convulsively as he found
is own release. He collapsed on top of her, his huge
rame jerking spasmodically, the rasping note of their
reathing the only sound in the stillness of the small
edroom.

Beth did not want to move ever again. Still joined to
Dex, she lay and wondered at the miracle she had ex-
erienced. None of the books she had read, or any girl-
alk, had prepared her for the absolute awesome glory
f making love, and she did love Dex. She moved her
rms around under his, stroking up his back and hugging
im to her. His glorious weight, the heavy pounding of
is heart—every move he made was a source of delight
o her. For a long time she held him, glorying in her
ove, completely forgetting the reality of the situation,
ntil suddenly Dex rolled over onto his back.

'I need the bathroom. Where is it?' he grunted.

With his familiar weight gone and his prosaic words, the cold reality of her situation hit her like a bucket of iced water.

'Mine is a tiny apartment. I'm sure a man of your intellect will find it with no trouble.'

'Sarcasm does not become you, Beth.' Dex sat up, his muscular thigh pressed lightly against her side, and her face flamed as he leant over her to drop a swift kiss on her swollen lips. 'Besides, my little innocent, these things are not reusable, and I have a feeling you and I are not finished yet.'

It was only then she realised he had used protection. Her face turned beetroot-red, as did the rest of her body, and, grabbing at the sheet, she pulled it haphazardly up over her naked body.

'Too late, Beth, I've seen it all,' Dex drawled with mocking amusement, and, completely uncaring of his nudity, he stood up.

Her fascinated gaze slid over his broad shoulders, his wide chest, still glistening with sweat, and, lower, to where his manhood nestled in a dense black brush of hair, and down his long, long legs. He was a magnificent male animal, even if he did have the character of a pig. No—that was probably insulting the pig, Beth thought, but she couldn't tear her eyes away from his naked form.

'But you have a good look, Beth. To my surprise and delight, you have no experience of men at all.' And he laughed out loud as she turned even redder with embarrassment. Lowering her gaze, she burnt with anger and humiliation.

CHAPTER SIX

ANGER won.... A furious Beth picked up a pillow and
threw it at Dex's retreating back, but it slid harmlessly
down the door to the floor as he vanished into the tiny
hall where the door to the bathroom was situated. The
sound of his laughter echoing in the quiet of her room
only infuriated her further.

She clenched her small hands together in impotent
fury and glanced wildly around her bedroom. She looked
down at her entwined hands and suddenly the enormity
of what had happened hit her like a punch in the stomach. She was naked, the bed was a rumpled mess, and
that hateful man was in her tiny bathroom and would be
back any second.

Blind panic engulfed her. She leapt out of bed and
dashed to the wardrobe, from where she dragged out a
blue woollen dressing gown and scrambled into it. Tying
the belt firmly around her waist, she stuck her feet into
a pair of old slippers in the shape of two basset-hounds.
Her eyes caught the glimpse of red on the floor, and
viciously she kicked her skirt and camisole under the
bed. She would never wear the outfit again, Beth vowed.
Then, another emotion lending her wings, she was out
of the room, across the small hall and into her living
room in a trice.

She had to get rid of Dex. That was the only thought
in her head as mechanically she walked into the kitchen
and switched on the electric kettle. She needed a drink,
a cup of coffee, to calm her shattered nerves. But she

had an awful premonition that it would take a lot more than a few cups of coffee to make her forget Dex and the turbulent feelings he had awakened in her tonight.

The kettle boiled, and, opening the cupboard where she stored her crockery, Beth took down a porcelain mug and spooned a large dollop of coffee granules into it from the jar of instant coffee on the bench. She couldn't stop her hand from shaking as she added the water, spilling some on the worktop. Reaction was setting in. But she refused to give in to it and, gritting her teeth, willed her hands to stop shaking. She opened the fridge, took out the milk, poured some milk in the mug and then added two generous spoons of sugar; she needed the energy, she told herself, to face Dex.

Dex! Beth stifled a groan of pure anguish. A few hours ago she had been the happiest girl in the world, engaged to the man she loved and eagerly anticipating going to bed with him. Well, she was no longer engaged to Dex, but she had been to bed with him. And now she felt like the stupidest, dumbest girl in the world. She couldn't find words to describe her own self-loathing. Naive did not begin to cover it...

But, a wicked voice whispered in her head, she was no longer naive in some respects. She had succumbed to his lovemaking with a wild passion she had not known she was capable of. A vivid image of his huge naked body entwined with hers had Beth reaching desperately for the coffee mug.

She took a great gulp of the hot coffee. How could she face him? Before she could answer her own question, the door swung open and Dex appeared. She glanced across at him, her huge green eyes warily following him as in a few lithe strides he covered the space between them, filling her small kitchen with his towering presence. He was dressed again, after a fashion. His jacket hung open across his broad chest and the silk shirt beneath fell loosely over the outside of his trousers. He looked what he was: a man who had just slaked his sexual appetite with his lady. His black hair was a tangle of curls over his broad forehead.

Beth blinked and glanced down, but seeing her ridiculous doggy slippers did nothing for her confidence. 'Damn Dex to hell...' she muttered under her breath. He had no right to look so virile, so disgustingly smug, and what had taken him so long in the bathroom? The inconsequential thought popped in her mind.

Glancing back up, she stiffened. His slate-grey eyes sought and captured hers, and his sensuous lips parted over perfect white teeth in a knowing, roguish smile.

'I'll take a cup of coffee, Beth, as it appears, by your hasty exit from the bedroom, that nothing more is on offer.'

Beth slammed her coffee mug down on the bench, the sheer gall of the man taking her breath away. Any faint hope that had lingered in her subconscious mind that maybe she could forgive him and they could stay together vanished. What Dex had just said convinced her absolutely she was not in his league, and could never in a million years inhabit his sophisticated world. She stared at him with wide angry eyes, as though she was seeing him for the first time.

What she saw was a devastatingly attractive, one-hundred-per cent powerful male animal—'animal' being the operative word. He had the sensitivity of a rhinoceros. It didn't matter a jot to him that he had seduced her and taken her virginity. In fact, according to Dex, he could take her, or a cup of coffee...either would do!

'Beth, are you all right?'

All right! she would never be all right again, but what the hell did he care? Fury such as Beth had never known flooded her whole being.

'Fine. I'm fine,' she snapped. 'But as for you, you can get out of here now, this minute. I don't want to see your conceited, arrogant face again as long as I live.'

Dex moved closer. 'Don't,' she said, holding her hands up to ward him off. 'Don't you dare come near me. Haven't you done enough damage for one night?'

Dex's eyes burned into hers. 'You don't mean that, Beth,' he said thickly, and reached for her. 'You're upset, emotional; it affects some girls like that the first time.' His hands closed over her shoulders and he pulled her to him. 'But the next time will be better, I promise.'

Beth almost choked. 'There is not going to be a next time, you great oaf. I don't want anything to do with you. I told you that an hour ago, but did you listen? No. You forced yourself on me.'

'Forced you! You were with me all the way,' he exclaimed, catching her chin and tilting her head back. 'You were begging for it.'

'No.' She shook her head. 'You forced me into it.'

His fingers tightened on her chin, his grey eyes narrowing to angry slits on her flushed, furious face. 'Don't lie, Beth. You wanted me, you know you did, and I asked you every step of the way; you only had to say no.'

Tears stung her eyes, whether of anger or regret, she didn't know. She pushed his hand from her chin and closed her eyes for a second, breathing deeply to regain her self-control.

Beth didn't see the bitter anguish in his eyes as he looked at her downbent head and then stepped back.

She opened her eyes and raised her head. 'I tried,' she declared bluntly.

They stared at each other, the tension in the air electric. The anger in his eyes made Beth quake inwardly, but she refused to show her feelings. Then, abruptly, Dex straightened his broad shoulders; his lips narrowing in a tight line, his handsome face expressionless, he clasped her elbow in his strong hand.

'If you really think that, Beth, then we have to talk.'

'No.' She wrenched her arm free. 'I have nothing, absolutely nothing I want to say to you. Except, get out of my home and out of my life.'

Dex was silent for a long moment, watching her with narrowed eyes. 'I don't get it,' he said curtly. 'You break our engagement. Then you melt in my arms. Then you accuse me of forcing you into it and demand I leave?'

'So, go!' she cried, her throat closing up as his hard grey eyes came to rest on her swollen lips.

'Oh, no,' Dex drawled. 'Not until I have made you swallow your lies.'

Beth's eyes rounded as he suddenly drew her against him, one hand sliding around her tiny waist, the other cupping the back of her head.

'I don't lie,' she croaked, just as his mouth covered hers and his hand tightened on her waist. His thrusting tongue searched the moist cavern of her mouth with a sensual ease that overcame her pathetic attempt to resist him in an instant. Her tongue touched his and white-hot passion sent the blood pounding through her veins.

When his mouth finally lifted from hers, she moaned and stared helplessly up at him, her lips parted, red and pouting, her lower body pressing into his hard thighs with a desire she could not disguise.

Dex smiled, a devastatingly wicked twist of his mobile mouth. 'Force? I think not, my sweet Beth. You are mine for the taking,' he said in a dry voice.

Where she got the strength to push him away, she did not know. Maybe it was just one humiliation too much for her pride to take. But shove him away she did.

'So maybe "force" was too strong a word,' she said in a surprisingly calm voice, when her insides were shaking. 'But if you didn't force me, you certainly coerced me.'

'And you loved every minute. I have your claw-marks on my back to prove it,' he drawled silkily.

'Maybe so, but it was just sex, and I will probably have sex with a lot more men in the future. No big deal,' she said with a shrug of her shoulders.

She shot a quick glance at his face, and to her surprise she saw guilt and some other indefinable emotion on his harshly handsome features.

'Your prerogative, of course. You're a beautiful girl, and you obviously have a talent for sex. But—'

'Thank you,' she cut in sharply, with a voice dripping in sarcasm. He thought she had a talent for sex. Was that supposed to be a compliment? A red haze of rage blurred her vision. 'But I don't need your no doubt expert opinion. I simply need you to leave. What was it you said so crudely earlier? "I didn't know whether to jilt you or jump you." But it wasn't quite like that, was it, Mr High-and-Mighty-Giordanni? You jumped me, but I've been trying for the past two hours to jilt you, and for a sophisticated man you're being remarkably obtuse—you just will not get the message.'

'I got your message long ago, Beth. You're a gold-digging little tease.' He squared his massive shoulders, his silver eyes narrowed on her lovely face. 'Hanging on to your virginity as a bankable asset, hoping to sell yourself to the wealthiest bidder. But this time you tried it on with the wrong man.'

His last insult was too much for Beth's fragile self-control. Shaking with fury, she raised her arm and landed a cracking slap on his tanned cheek with the palm of her hand.

'Take that, you bastard, and get out,' she spat.

Dex lifted a large hand to rub the side of his face; with his other hand he clasped her wrist in an iron grip. The air crackled with undisguised animosity. She must have been insane to have ever felt she loved this man, she thought, as she furiously stared into his eyes.

'If you were a man I would kill you,' Dex offered, with a silky menace that made her blood run cold. 'But, in the circumstances, given your emotional state, I will allow you the one slap.'

Magnanimous swine... He would "allow" her... It was the final straw for Beth. Her head ached, her heart ached, her throat ached with the effort of holding back the tears. If Dex didn't leave in a minute, she would break down.

Her shoulders slumped, her head bent and she muttered desolately, 'Please get out.' Amazingly, when Beth lifted her head again, it was to see Dex walking to the front door, and with some spark of her pride rising in her exhausted brain, she yelled, 'Take your ring with you. It's around there somewhere.'

With a sense of *déjà vue* she watched as Dex once again turned around in the doorway. His eyes flicked briefly over her, his face a mask of total indifference. 'You keep it, Beth.' And with a flippant shrug of his broad shoulders, he added, 'You've earned it now.' With that parting shot, he walked out of her apartment and out of her life. Or so Beth thought...

* * *

Horrified, Beth looked at her reflection in the bathroom mirror. Oh, my God! I can't go to work looking like this. Her eyes were red-rimmed and sore, her lips still swollen from Dex's kisses. She looked an absolute mess. Hardly surprising, she thought bitterly, she hadn't slept a wink. After Dex had left, the tears she had held at bay for what had seemed like an eternity had started to fall.

Giving in to her grief, she had cried until she'd thought she had no tears left. Then she had taken a long, vigorous shower, determined to wash every trace of Dex from her flesh, and had tried to go to bed. But the sight of her rumpled bed, the scent of Dex lingering on the bed linen, had brought on a fresh bout of tears. Eventually she had curled up in her armchair and stared sightlessly into the dark living room, remembering every smile, every touch, every single second she had spent with Dex. Every lying word...

For once in her life Beth had been able to appreciate her wayward mother. If Leanora had suffered like this at every break-up, she must have the heart of a lion. Beth had never felt pain like it, had never realised mental pain could be so powerful... Her chest physically ached, her stomach churned, but, worse, her faith in herself as a woman, a valued human being, was almost destroyed. Dexter Giordanni had taken away her confidence, along with her virginity, by his deceit. She'd curled up in a small ball in the chair, hugging her knees, and wished she was dead.

The chiming of a clock in the distance had finally roused her from the well of self-pity and anguish. Six in the morning. Brushing the mass of hair from her eyes, she had got stiffly out of the chair and went to the bathroom.

Beth grimaced at her reflection once more, and headed

for the bedroom. Her heart squeezed at the sight of her bed, the covers a tangled mass, as she had left them last night. From somewhere she got the strength to rip off all the linen and shove it into the wicker basket in the bathroom. She refused to recognise the musky scent of their lovemaking, or the lingering trace of Dex's after-shave on the sheets. Five minutes later, she'd dressed in a plain black skirt and yellow sweater and was marching into the kitchen.

Hadn't she read somewhere that a slice of raw potato on one's eyes revitalised them? Quickly making a cup of coffee, she gulped it down, and then, finding a potato in the vegetable rack, she sliced it. Returning to the living room, she sank down into the armchair and plopped the two pieces of potato on her eyes. The tiniest hint of a smile twitched her full lips as she imagined what she must look like, and suddenly she realised that life must go on, and that it could be good again. She would laugh again. Maybe it would take a while—not maybe, certainly. But she was not about to let a man like Dexter Giordanni destroy her life.

Her determination was sorely tested when she walked into the building that housed the offices of Canary Characters. Every employer had to sign in as a security precaution, and as soon as Beth leaned over the reception desk to do just that, Lizzie, the receptionist, noticed Beth was not wearing her ring.

'Hi, Beth. Lost the rock already?' Lizzie asked jokingly.

Beth felt the colour rising in her face, but she forced herself to respond equally flippantly, 'The man, yes. The rock, no...'

'Oh, Beth!' Lizzie exclaimed. 'You mean, your engagement is off?'

'Yes. I'm free and single once again.' And, having signed her name, she straightened up and had to look at Lizzie, and the pity she saw in the girl's eyes made her cringe.

'Beth, I am so sorry.'

'Don't be. I'm not. I got to keep the ring—an investment for my old age.' She made herself grin before turning away, then crossed to the elevator that took her to the drawing office.

Lizzie's comment was not the first. By the end of the day, everyone from the director down knew Beth was no longer engaged. The comments varied from sympathy from most of the female members of the staff to jokes from a good proportion of the men. They ranged from 'The briefest engagement in the West', to an offer to 'ring the *Guinness Book of Records*, no pun intended, and register the shortest engagement in the world'.

Only Mary, her friend, didn't believe Beth's unconcerned attitude. Cornering her in the washroom, she asked, 'What really happened, Beth?'

Beth longed to lean on Mary's shoulder and confide the whole sordid business to her. Pride alone made her say, 'You were right, Mary. Whirlwind romances don't work. Dex and I shared a few kisses. He gave me a ring and I thought it was love. But yesterday, when I met him again after not seeing him for a few days, we both realised there was nothing there, no chemistry.'

God forgive her the lie, she thought. Remembering Dex's kisses was enough to make her ache all over.

'If you say so, but remember, if you need a shoulder to cry on, or someone to confide in, I'm here for you.'

Beth gave Mary a trembling smile. 'I know, but really I'll be okay.'

*   *   *

Surprisingly, at the end of two weeks she almost *was* okay. Setting the small table in her kitchen for three people one evening, she actually found herself humming the latest hit tune. Mike was bringing his girlfriend, Elizabeth, over to meet Beth and have a meal, and later the three of them were going on to a Hallowe'en party. Beth was looking forward to it. Plus, she thanked her lucky stars she hadn't seen Mike since their cabaret act together, and consequently he knew nothing of her brief engagement. So there would be no awkward questions.

Her broken engagement had been barely a three-day wonder at the office. And by throwing herself into her work she'd had little time to think of Dex. Which was just as well, because she had heard not a word from the man. The ring he had given her she had found on the living room floor and stuck in the back of her dressing table drawer, unable to look at it.

It was the nights that were the problem. Alone in her apartment, her traitorous mind would relive the moments she had spent in Dex's embrace. She kept telling herself his every kiss had been a lie. But it didn't stop her body flooding with heat as she lay in her bed, remembering Dex sharing it with her.

Sleep, when it came, was restless... His face filled her dreams, and sometimes his whole body. On those nights she would wake up in the middle of the night, her body wet with sweat and aching with frustration.

But tonight, Beth promised herself, as she stood in front of the bathroom mirror, carefully applying thick black eye make-up, tonight would be different. She was going to start socialising again, having fun, even if it killed her. Knowing her stepbrother, if anyone could make her laugh, Mike could.

The doorbell rang and she hurried to answer it. Beth

opened the door and a smile of pure pleasure covered her face. Then she burst out laughing.

'Mike, that is you?' she asked, when she managed to stop chuckling. He was wearing a skeleton costume: black from neck to toe, with luminous ivory paint outlining the bone structure.

'Who else, sis? Allow me to introduce you to Elizabeth,' and Beth gasped again as Mike walked into the centre of the room with the most hideous-looking creature on his arm!

Beth immediately liked the girl. Any woman who had the nerve to meet her boyfriend's sister for the first time dressed in a witch's costume had to be a fun person.

'Delighted to meet you.' Beth grinned, and was struck by the laughing blue eyes that smiled back at her—even if they were set in a face that sported a huge crooked false nose, a mouth with half the teeth blacked out and a large wart on the chin.

'Hello, Beth, and let me say straight off this was Mike's idea.' The girl's eyes turned to Mike, and they smiled at each other.

The look of pure togetherness that passed between the couple made Beth's heart ache, and it hurt even more when Mike caught the girl's hand and held it out for Beth to admire.

'You're the first to know, Beth. Elizabeth and I got engaged last night.'

The ring was beautiful, a brilliant blue sapphire surrounded by diamonds, and Beth congratulated them both, brushing away a tear as she did so.

'And that's not all, Beth.' I was promoted on Monday to sales director, at almost double my present salary.'

'Ah, so I get back all the money I've lent you over the years,' Beth teased.

'Hey, hang on, sis! I haven't got the money yet, but my credit rating has soared.'

Elizabeth shook her head and gave Beth a wry smile, and they both burst out laughing.

The tone for the evening was set; amidst much laughter, the three of them ate the meal Beth had prepared of spaghetti *al guanciale* and crusty garlic bread. The party they were going to didn't start until ten, and as they were taking a taxi, the champagne Mike had brought with him was was soon finished, along with the bottle Beth had originally bought to share with Dex. With the bottle empty, Beth thought whimsically, she had finally closed the lid on the Dex episode.

Mike insisted on opening another bottle of wine, but Beth had had enough and made coffee, then served it in the living room.

Elizabeth and Mike shared her only armchair, and Beth curled up on a large red bean bag.

'So, Beth, you've heard all my news. How's life treating you?' Mike suddenly asked, and, not waiting for her reply, he grinned and added, 'You actually *look* like a cat curled up on that cushion. But don't you think it's time you bought some more furniture?'

Beth meowed very convincingly. 'My whiskers are in the bathroom.' Her cat costume consisted of a black bodysuit with a long tail, and a hood with two ears attached to cover her hair. 'I'll go and stick them on now,' she said, ignoring his questions and leaping to her feet. Beth knew Mike, and she knew before long he would get back to quizzing her about her private life, and she wasn't sure she could handle it.

Ten minutes later, Beth pranced back into the living room and did a pirouette. 'So, am I a cat? Or what?' she said with a smile. With the hood covering her bright hair, and long whiskers glued to her top lip, she looked every inch the black cat of myth.

'Cat? No.'

'No?' Beth looked at Mike, her smile vanishing. 'I thought the costume was good.'

'Kitten, maybe. You're so tiny,' Mike mocked, knowing just how to rile her.

'Fiend!' Beth cried, and made a leap for him, her hands outstretched like claws.

Elizabeth slid off the arm of the chair as Beth set about tickling Mike. She knew it was his pet hate, as her lack of height was hers, and in the ensuing uproar she didn't hear the intercom.

It was Elizabeth's voice that finally registered.

'I've told him to come up, Beth. Okay?'

Rolling onto the floor, Beth stood up straight. 'Told who? What?' She turned her puzzled gaze on Elizabeth, who was standing by the door.

'Dexter Giordanni. He said he was a friend of yours, and as Mike has mentioned doing business with the man, I guessed it was all right.'

'What?' Beth exclaimed in horror.

'Why, you sly dog, Beth. Or should that be cat?' Mike said, grinning from ear to ear. 'You're dating the great man himself.'

'No, I am not!' she snapped, just as the doorbell rang and Elizabeth went to open the front door.

Beth's green-eyed gaze shot to the man who stood in the living-room doorway. She couldn't move; she was frozen in shock. Dex was looking around in much the same state of shock.

'*Dio*, what is this? A mad house?' His startled gaze swept over the witch, the skeleton rising from the armchair, and finally settled on the cat.

Mike came to the rescue with his usual light-hearted manner. 'Come in, come in,' he told Dex, and then proudly introduced his fiancée, Elizabeth.

Elizabeth took one look at the tall, dark, handsome man, dressed in a formal black dinner suit and snowy white shirt, and turned on Mike.

'I knew I shouldn't have let you talk me into this costume. I look a sight.'

Beth wasn't surprised at Elizabeth's reaction. It was one thing to appear a freak to the man who loved you. But quite another to meet a very handsome stranger.

But Dex cut in. 'No, really, Elizabeth, you look absolutely stunning. I have never seen a better-looking witch.'

His deep velvet voice, threaded with amusement, grated along Beth's nerves. She watched him smile down into Elizabeth's face, her lips curling in distaste.

'Or a more lively skeleton.' He shared a grin with Mike. 'And as for the cat...' He turned his amused gaze on Beth as he walked towards her. 'I don't believe I have ever seen a more perfect feline.' His grey eyes raked her from head to toe, and she bristled, much like the animal she was pretending to be.

The smooth stretch-fur fabric moulded to every inch of her firm young body like a second skin, and Dex's blatant appraisal, the way his eyes lingered a shade too long on her high, full breasts, brought a furious flush to her small face. When he finally looked into her face, her green eyes flared back at him, shooting sparks of furious hostility.

'How dare you come here?' Beth breathed, keeping her voice low, so Mike and Elizabeth would not hear.

'The costume was made for you, Beth, darling. So appropriate,' Dex drawled, loud enough for the neighbours to hear, Beth thought bitterly, and then to her astonishment he caught her by the shoulders and lowered his dark head. She thought for a terrifying minute he was going to kiss her, but his lips grazed her cheek. 'And I still have the scratch-marks to prove it,' he whispered, for her ears only.

Beth blushed even redder. A vivid image of Dex's large naked body covering hers flashed in her mind's eye, and her own stupid reaction, her slender arms clinging to him as if her life depended on it. Angry with herself, and him, she pulled out of his hold.

Deliberately sidestepping Dex, and focusing her attention on her stepbrother, she said, 'Come on, Mike, we had better get going or we'll be late.' Safely in reach of the door, she dared to look at Dex again.

'Nice to see you again, Dex, but, as you can see, we're on our way out. Perhaps you can ring me the next time you're in town.'

'Yes, I will do that,' he said suavely, walking towards the door.

Beth opened the door for him with a polite smile on her face, tinged with a profound relief that he was leaving. She glanced at the keys in her hand, and realised she could hardly carry a bag.

'Give them to me, Beth,' Elizabeth suggested, seeing her dilemma. 'I'm the only one with pockets, as Mike so readily informed me when it came to paying the taxi fare on the way over.'

'That's Mike,' Beth said with a laugh, handing the keys over, and was complacently congratulating herself on her adult handling of the situation, even if her stomach felt as if a horde of butterflies had taken control of it, when Mike decided to get in on the act...

CHAPTER SEVEN

How it had happened, Beth did not know. One minute she was showing Dexter Giordanni out of her door, and half an hour later the same man was helping her out of his limousine while Mike and Elizabeth were already halfway down the steps to the open door of Mike's old college friend's restaurant in Holland Park. The restaurant was closed to the general public for the night in order to host the private Hallowe'en party.

Shrugging Dex's hand off her arm, she snarled, 'I don't need your help, thank you very much.'

Stuck in the back seat of the car, with Dex on one side and Mike on the other, it had been the journey from hell for Beth. Unable to complain at Mike's high-handed attitude in inviting Dex to accompany them to the party, she had silently fumed. The close proximity of Dex's large body had only infuriated her further. Much as she hated to admit it, his closeness, his warmth, the familiar scent of him, had set every nerve in her body on red alert.

'Temper, temper, Beth. There's no need to play the part of the spitting cat quite so enthusiastically,' he opined, grinning down at her.

'And there's no need for you to be here,' she shot back, wanting to knock the smile off his handsome face. 'You could easily have said no to Mike's invitation. You're not in fancy dress, and you'll stand out like a sore thumb. It's not your scene at all,' she ranted on.

But Dex silenced her by placing a long finger over her mouth.

'My scene or not, I could not desert you in your hour of need.'

Beth's eyes widened in puzzlement. 'My need?' What on earth was he talking about? She needed Dex like a hole in the head! She was still fighting to recover from their last disastrous encounter.

'I pride myself on being a gentleman, and it was obvious you did not have a date for the evening. You know what they say: Two's company, three's a crowd. I had to step in and save you any embarrassment.'

His mock concern raised her temperature another notch. 'Why, you patronising prig! If I had wanted an escort for the evening, I could have had one.'

'If you say so. But let us get inside; we are holding up the traffic.'

Only then did Beth notice the cars drawn up behind Dex's limousine, and about a dozen people approaching. Before she could think of a suitable retort, Dex slipped his arm around her waist and urged her down the steps and into the foyer. She knew he was winding her up deliberately, and belatedly she thought of an answer.

'I didn't have an escort because I didn't want one. I intend to play the field tonight,' she declared, with a casual sophistication she did not feel. At barely five feet two, and dressed as a cat with whiskers, sophisticated she was not... Anyway, it was a lie. Actually, all she really wanted to do was run home. But she refused to give Dex the satisfaction of knowing how much seeing him again had upset her.

'I am in the field,' Dex murmured, swinging her around in his arms and holding her close against his large body. 'Play with me,' he drawled huskily, his grey eyes narrowed intently on her face.

Beth swallowed hard. There was no mistaking the flare of desire in the depths of his eyes as one large hand slid down her back and pressed her hard against his muscular thighs.

Beth glanced wildly around. She tried to ease away, but it wasn't that simple. The small restaurant entrance was a mass of bodies, from ghosts to devils, druids—and drunks, by the look of it, as one particularly plump man, in what looked like a nightshirt, fell against her.

'Come on.' Dex's hand dropped from her waist and, curving a protective arm around her slender shoulders, hauling her hard into his side, he guided her through the crush of people into the large dining room where there was a lot more space.

Intensely aware of his thigh brushing against her hip, and his hand on her shoulder, it took all Beth's willpower to repress the shiver his touch ignited.

'I'm all right now,' she said curtly, slipping out from under his arm and glancing around.

Beth's green eyes widened incredulously at the scene before her. On a platform at one end of the room, a disc jockey dressed in a red Spandex suit, a cape and horns—the devil incarnate!—was doing his stuff. The music was loud, and multi-coloured flashing strobe lights cast weird and wonderful shadows over the centre of the room, where a couple of dozen people dressed as demons, witches and warlocks, and some very scantily clad women, gyrated in time to the beat... Around the sides, people lounged at tables, drinking and laughing. It reminded her of an oil painting she had seen in the Tate Gallery by a seventeenth-century Italian master, depicting hell.

The irony of it did not escape her. Hell was exactly how she felt. Acutely conscious of Dex's brooding presence beside her, she glanced up at him and had the terrible conviction that unless she escaped from this party pretty, damn quick, hell was where she was destined to stay!

'Your stepbrother certainly has some interesting friends,' Dex commented, one dark brow arching sardonically as he looked around the room.

Beth followed his superior gaze to where it rested on a particularly voluptuous woman, who appeared to be wearing three fig leaves and nothing else. What the brief costume had to do with Hallowe'en, Beth could not imagine. But, glancing back at Dex, she let her lips twist in a cynical smile. Obviously the girl in question knew why. Dex was drooling. How typical, Beth thought bitterly, and took the chance to edge away from him.

Catching sight of Mike and Elizabeth, she made her way towards them. Suddenly a sharp tug on the tail of her costume had her falling back against a rock-hard body. Fighting to retain her balance, she squirmed around and found herself staring at Dex's shirt-front. She put her hands flat against his broad chest and tried to push him away.

'Will you let go of my tail?' she snapped. Why, oh, why had she let herself be talked into wearing this ridiculous costume?

'But you have such a nice tail, Beth.' Her furious green eyes clashed with his and she saw the devilment lurking in their silver depths. She felt his hand twisting the offending appendage around his wrist until his palm settled firmly over her bottom, and she knew damn well it was not the tail of her costume he was talking about.

'In fact, I love your costume. Cats are my favourite

animal.' His other hand stroked slowly, very deliberately, down her spine, making her shudder. 'It is *purrfect* for you,' he teased huskily. Well aware of her involuntary reaction to his blatant caress, tossing back his head, he laughed out loud at the expression of frustrated fury twisting her delicate features.

His laughter, the flash of his brilliant white teeth, was too much for Beth.

'Add a pair of white fangs to your big mouth, and, hey presto! The perfect Count Dracula!' she spat back.

He pulled her closer, one hand easing up her back to clasp the back of her head, untangling the tail of her costume and settling his other arm more firmly around her, if such a thing was possible.

'Count Dracula. I like that, Beth.' His hand slid to the nape of her neck and she felt the pressure of his long fingers on her throat.

'Especially if you let me kiss your neck,' he declared outrageously, his eyes glittering with wickedly sensual intent on her flushed face.

The pulse in her neck leapt beneath his fingers; her body flooded with heat. She swallowed hard, the erotic image he had created swamping her mind. Her hands on his chest, supposedly to push him away, lingered against the soft silk of his shirt. She felt his hard thighs stirring against her, and was made shockingly aware of the man in the most primitive way possible. She opened her mouth to speak but no sound came out as his dark head bent and his mouth bit gently, then sucked, on the only bit of flesh exposed by her all-encompassing costume: her throat.

She went weak at the knees, a low moan escaping through her parted lips. Dex moved slightly, his long legs splayed, and he pulled her close between his thighs.

His hands tightened on her buttocks and back. What would have happened next? Beth did not dare contemplate it as Mike saved her from making a complete fool of herself.

'You two dancing, or what?' His cheerful voice echoed on the fringes of Beth's mind.

Dex lifted his dark head and grinned at Mike. 'Dancing—now—thanks to you.' Swirling Beth around, he deftly manoeuvred her into the crowd of dancers.

Mortified, her face burning, Beth stiffened in his arms, wishing with all her heart she was anywhere else but here. Not strictly true, a little voice echoed in her head. Being held close to Dex, his male warmth enfolding her, was as near to heaven as a woman could get.

Fool, she told herself. Dex didn't really want her. He had taken her out in the first place to keep her away from Paul Morris, the man his sister wanted. He had taken her to bed to prove he could, and she, weak-willed wimp that she was, had let him. How cold-blooded could a man get?

She sighed; the pressure of his hand on her back and the subtle movement of his body against hers was anything but cold, in fact it was the reverse. She frowned in concentration, worried that if she relaxed for a second she would find herself caving into him. She silently cursed her stupid costume yet again. A fine layer of stretch jersey was no protection against the powerful appeal of Dex's muscle-packed body. Her breasts hardened, the nipples rigid against the fine jersey. She didn't know whether to press herself against him to disguise her arousal or pull away from him and take the risk of revealing her vulnerable state.

'Don't worry, Beth. It will put premature lines on your beautiful face.'

His warm breath caressed her brow, and at the softly drawled words her head jerked back in surprise. The damn man could read her mind.

'So what? You won't be around to see them,' she said, shooting him a dismissive glance.

Dex grinned. 'I wouldn't be too sure, Beth.' His grey eyes gleamed with mocking amusement as he held her slightly away from him and added, 'Your delectable body tells a different story.'

'Don't flatter yourself,' she muttered, 'it's the heat. This catsuit is like a strait-jacket.'

Dex chuckled. '"Straight" is hardly how I would describe you.' His glance swept over her slender curves in frank masculine appreciation, and his chuckle changed to outright laughter.

Words failed her. He might find the situation highly amusing, but she was mortified. If he laughed at her once more she would hit him. But cold common sense told her that sparring with Dex was a losing game. Dancing was probably a whole lot safer than trying to argue with him in this crowd. Relaxing slightly against him, she felt his arms tighten around her. It felt so good, and, if she was honest, it was where she wanted to be. With a soft sigh she buried her head on his chest and gave herself up to the music.

Beth liked dancing, and for a large man Dex was amazingly light on his feet. They moved around the floor in perfect unison, not speaking, simply swaying to the sounds of the music. The seductive power of his body had Beth, against all her better intentions, melting against him.

The tempo of the music changed to a heavy jungle beat, and Dex bent low so that his breath brushed her cheek. 'Do you want to continue?'

'Yes.' Why not? she thought. It was a party and she deserved some fun, and, slipping out of his arms, she began to gyrate with the music. Her green eyes clashed with his. 'If you can,' she goaded him. And he could...

He danced the same way as he did everything—perfectly. She should have guessed. Beth had thought him the sexiest man on two legs before, but watching his long body move with sinuous grace to the heavy beat was a lesson in eroticism that made her respond in kind.

As if by some unspoken agreement for the next half-hour or more they danced, and laughed, and teased each other with their bodies in perfect harmony. When eventually the music returned to a slow beat and Dex pulled her into his arms, Beth went willingly.

'My little cat, my fantasy,' he murmured against the top of her head. His hands stroked up and down her arms, one hand finally settling at the base of her spine, holding her tightly against him, and his other hand curving around her chin and tilting her head back. 'Will you purr for me, Beth?' he asked, his dark eyes intent on her flushed face. 'Fulfil my fantasy?'

'My turn, I think.' Mike's voice cut in before Beth could answer.

'Okay...' Dex said, his hand falling from her chin and turning her deftly towards Mike. 'I'll go and find us all a drink.' He was in complete control in a second, while Beth was fighting for breath.

Beth didn't know whether to be grieved or relieved as Mike whirled her around the floor. 'Why the haste, brother dear?' she managed to get out when she had recovered enough to speak.

Stopping dead at the edge of the dance floor, Mike looked straight at her and demanded, 'What exactly is going on between you and Giordanni?'

'Nothing. Nothing at all.'

'This is Mike, your brother. I know you, and I remember the gooey-eyed look you had after you met the man at the boss's party. So what gives? Have you been dating him ever since?'

'Don't be silly. I went out with him a couple of times, and realised he wasn't my type. I haven't seen him for weeks.'

'So why is he almost devouring you on the dance floor? And why did he call at your apartment tonight?'

'Mike, you're beginning to sound like Big Brother with all your questions. I have no idea why Giordanni called at my apartment, and I don't really care.'

But she did care, and she couldn't believe her own oversight. She had spent the last hour with the man actually enjoying herself, if she was honest, and it had never occurred to her to ask Dex why he had called. She had to pull herself together. So far she had been reacting, not acting.

'Sorry. But according to Elizabeth you needed rescuing. Don't ask me why. "Women's intuition," she said, and, as her wish is my command, consider yourself rescued,' Mike informed her with a wry smile.

'You're a fool, but I love you.' She was touched by his protective attitude.

'As long as you're not a fool over Giordanni.' Mike's blue-eyed gaze was suddenly serious. 'He is a handsome devil, and I know he's a brilliant businessman, but his reputation with the ladies is the pits.'

'Who are you maligning now, fiancé mine?' Elizabeth arrived and tucked her arm through Mike's.

Beth glanced around the room, her eyes widening on the voluptuous lady, who was now exposing one breast, and shot quickly back at Elizabeth. 'The rather lively lady who has just lost a fig leaf,' she improvised, and immediately the attention of Mike and Elizabeth was diverted to the dance floor, much to Beth's relief. The disc jockey was yelling it was midnight, over the music, and the crowd was going wild.

'Oh, my God. Don't you dare look, Mike,' Elizabeth exclaimed, putting her hands over her fiancé's eyes, and laughing with Beth over his shoulder.

'Spoilsport!' Mike cried.

'Here, have a drink and cool down.' Dex's deep voice joined the conversation. Beth spun around to find him standing behind her, miraculously carrying four glasses of champagne in his large hands.

They all took a glass. Beth drank hers straight off; she needed it. She had been perilously close to forgetting why she had left Dex in the first place, and she hated her own weakness.

Suddenly she found the noise was deafening. Her head was beginning to ache, and the hood of her costume was feeling tighter by the minute. She glanced up at Dex. He was hovering over her like a vampire bat, she thought, her imagination running riot. If she didn't escape soon, she would faint. Elizabeth was saying something, Beth knew, but she could barely hear above the noise.

'What did you say?' Beth asked, as Elizabeth and Mike put their empty glasses on a convenient table and hand in hand turned to Beth.

'This party is turning rather wild,' Mike said, sharing a very male look over the top of her head with Dex. 'We're leaving.' And, grabbing Elizabeth's hand, he set off for the exit.

Dex took her glass from her nerveless fingers and set it on the table. 'So are we.'

Arrogant, domineering swine... 'No, the party's just

warming up,' she challenged, not because she had any
desire to stay, but simply to thwart him. He was so damn
superior.

'If it gets any warmer, it will be illegal,' Dex replied.
Catching Beth's wrist in his large hand, he added, 'Mike
and Elizabeth need a ride home. Come on.'

And, weaving through the crowd, he dragged Beth
behind him.

Once out of the restaurant and in the fresh air, Dex
stopped at the foot of the steps leading up to street level.
'Are you all right? You look a bit pale.' He slanted her
a teasing grin. 'For a cat.'

'I'm fine.' Beth tore the hood from her head. She
hated the catsuit. She ran her fingers through her hair
and shook her head. The relief was unbelievable. With
part of her costume gone, part of her common sense
returned.

'But what about you? Why did you call at my apartment? Why did you come to this party? You could have
easily said no. What exactly are you playing at?' she
demanded, finally able to ask all the questions that had
been preying on her mind since Dex had walked back
into her life.

'Questions, questions. You'd better watch it, Beth.
Remember the saying. Curiosity killed the cat.' And he
laughed again.

Sick to death of his stupid cat jokes, she turned on
him. 'I wish I could kill *you*,' she said venomously, and,
pushing past him, she ran up the steps to the street.

Mike and Elizabeth were standing on the pavement
arm in arm, and Beth hastened to stand beside them. Dex
appeared a second later. He gave Beth a hard-eyed stare
but said not a word. A snap of his fingers and, by some
miracle, the limousine drew up alongside the kerb.

'Where to first?' Dex addressed the question to Mike.

'My place.' He looked at Dex and smiled as he gave the address. 'My new fiancée and I have a lot to discuss.'

'Drop me off first,' Beth said quickly, and looked at Dex too. He stared down at her with narrowed eyes, his expression unreadable.

'Let's leave it to the driver.' He said coolly, his hand at Beth's elbow urging her into the back of the car. Nobody argued with him...

Mike and Elizabeth were in a world of their own, arms around each other, whispering sweet nothings, and it was Beth's sheer bad luck that Mike's apartment was a whole lot nearer the restaurant than hers.

'Here.' Elizabeth handed Dex Beth's door keys. 'Look after her.' After a hasty goodnight, the couple quickly headed towards Mike's door.

It was obvious what they had in mind, and who could blame them? They were young and in love. But, unfortunately for Beth, it left her alone in the back seat of the car with Dex. Plus, the man had her door key.

They sat side by side in tense silence as the chauffeur drove through the city. Beth slanted Dex a sidelong glance and quickly looked away. He was bitterly angry. She could sense it, see it in the rigid lines of his hard face. Her nerves were pulled as taut as a bowstring—if she didn't get out of the car in a moment, she would scream.

She felt the tension increase with every passing mile, and breathed a sigh of relief when the limousine cruised quietly to a halt outside her apartment building. The chauffeur got out and, after walking around the front of the car, held open the door. Dex slid out and stood on the pavement, waiting for her.

He was simply being polite, Beth told herself, and slid

out after him. 'Thank you for a nice evening,' she said stiffly, 'give me my key, please.' She held out her hand, hoping to get away with the social niceties. But she didn't.

Taking the hand she offered, Dex ordered, 'Inside,' and dragged her across the foyer and into the lift.

'There's no need for you to accompany me,' Beth said firmly, refusing to be intimidated by his high-handed attitude.

He pressed the elevator button, turning to her with an icy expression in his steely eyes. 'I decide what is needed,' he stated. Pulling her out of the elevator, then into her apartment, he added chillingly, 'Not you. Not any more.'

Beth looked up as he closed and locked the door behind him. 'Exactly what do you mean by that?' she demanded, but she couldn't help edging away from him. There was something in his expression, his cold, aloof stance, that sent shivers down her spine.

Ignore him, her common sense told her. Ignore him, walk away, and he'll leave.

'I'm going to get changed.' Beth turned her back to him. 'See yourself out.' And she headed for the door that led into her bedroom. She half expected him to follow, but amazingly he didn't. She closed her bedroom door behind her and wished it had a lock. Then she heard a door slam; she couldn't believe her luck. But she was taking no chances. Quickly she picked up an old green sweatsuit, and dashed into the bathroom. The bathroom *did* have a lock.

She listened for any sound from the living room, but everything was quiet. Slipping out of the embarrassing costume, she sighed with relief and stepped into the baggy pants. She slipped the sweater over her head and

ran her fingers through her hair. Only then did she look
in the mirror. A brief smile curved her full mouth, and
she gave a grimace of pain as she pulled the whiskers
from her face.

No wonder Dex had gone, she thought, still grinning.
She looked an absolute sight. She thoroughly washed
and dried her face, removing all the exaggerated eye
make-up, and, picking up a hairbrush, briskly brought
her unruly auburn hair into some sort of order. Sighing
with relief, she saw she looked almost normal. She un-
locked the bathroom door. A cup of cocoa, and then
hopefully to bed and to sleep. She didn't want to think
about the evening's events.

She walked into the living room and stopped dead.
Dex was leaning against the small mantlepiece. He
looked up as she walked in. A flick of his lashes sent
his gaze skimming over her assessingly, noting the
baggy green sweatsuit with a wry smile.

'Hardly haute couture, but all that can change,' he
murmured, and she felt as though he was stripping her
with his eyes.

'I thought you'd gone,' she exclaimed.

Dex shrugged his broad shoulders in a typical Latin
gesture. 'No.'

'But I heard the door.' Beth was stunned, and it
showed. She looked at the hall door, and back at Dex.
He had loosened his tie and unfastened the first few buttons on his shirt. Thankfully he had not removed his
jacket; it still fit perfectly over his broad shoulders. One
hand was in his trouser pocket; the other was holding a
glass of wine.

'It was the kitchen door; I raided your refrigerator.
Drink?'

Then she saw the half-empty bottle of wine on the

mantlepiece and another glass. 'You—but…' Her mouth worked but she was too confused to get the words out.

'Sit down, Beth. Have a drink and listen. You asked me before why I called around here earlier. Before you decided you wished I was dead,' he reminded her cynically.

Looking down, she felt a brief flicker of shame, but it quickly expired as she watched him casually withdraw his hand from his pocket and pick up the other glass of wine from the mantlepiece. Stepping forward, he held it out towards her. 'Drink. You might need it.'

She was so surprised, she automatically reached out and took the glass. His long fingers brushed hers and she felt the contact right through to her shoulder.

'Why?' she muttered. She had suffered shock upon shock tonight, and her brain could not take it in.

'The simple answer is, I have a proposal for you.'

Taking a sip from her drink, she glanced over the rim of her glass. 'Go ahead,' she murmured. 'You will, anyway.' The cold determination in his grey eyes as they met hers was unmistakable.

'Usually I visit London twice a year at most, but since acquiring the casino—and more recently a trio of city centre hotels—I find I am going to have to spend a lot more time here. I'm a normal man, with normal needs, and I need a woman here. I want you to be that woman.'

Confused, she surveyed him. 'But I told you. I don't want to marry you.'

One dark brow arched quizzically, a ruthless smile curving his sensuous mouth. 'No more than I want to marry you. In fact, if you recall, I never actually asked you. I gave you a ring, a bauble. That was all.'

Embarrassment turned her face scarlet. Her only consolation was that at last he was speaking the truth. She had overheard him saying pretty much the same thing in the office that dreadful day. Forcing her turbulent thoughts into some kind of order, she tilted her head back and looked at him sharply.

Unease stirred inside her. There was something sinister in his austere features. 'I don't understand.' She shook her head. 'What do you mean?'

'Let me make it simple for you. I have bought an apartment in London and I want you to live in it. You can continue with your career—whatever. My only stipulation is, when I am in London you make yourself available at my convenience.'

Beth stared at him, her strained features reflecting her shock. Dex, the man she had thought she loved, was quite cold-bloodedly suggesting she live with him, albeit on a part-time basis. If she had not been so horrified, she would have been furious.

She searched Dex's harshly set features. He looked just as she imagined he would look when buying a casino or a company. His arrogance, his enormous conceit, took her breath away. But she was not in the market. Not for Dex. Not for any man.

Suddenly the black humour of the situation hit her. Of course she could see through his plan. Install Beth in his apartment and keep her away from Paul Morris. Obviously his sister was having some difficulty bringing Paul to heel.

'Why me?' she asked, wondering what kind of story he would come up with. She was sure it would not be the truth.

'I find after having had one bite of the cherry I have a burning desire to cultivate the rest of the tree,' he returned softly.

Beth had to repress a smile. He wasn't serious; he was simply trying it on. 'For a man whose first language isn't English, you have a great line in metaphors,' she quipped, letting the smile break through. Dex had wit, even if he was a devious devil.

But there was no corresponding smile from Dex. Instead he stepped towards her, a ruthless determination glinting in his narrowed eyes. 'So, is it a deal?'

It was unthinkable, but he actually was serious. Her body frozen with shock, Beth's eyes searched his face, looking for some indication that it was a joke. A Hallowe'en prank, maybe. But she could see nothing in his expression to allay her fear—fear for herself, because for a brief moment she had been tempted. The thought of once more experiencing the delights his magnificent body could give her had stirred an unwanted response inside her.

'No,' she said softly, whether denying herself or Dex, she wasn't sure. Then, as fury at his insulting proposition overcame her shock, she repeated forcefully, 'No! No, never in a million years!'

'So adamant, and so wrong.' His hand reached out and circled her throat, tilting her head up, and his eyes narrowed. 'I can feel the pulse beating madly in your throat. However much you try to hide it, you want me. You melt when I touch you. It is the same for me. Our relationship will be a mutually fulfilling affair.'

She opened her mouth to deny it and his dark head bent, his mouth taking hers. She shuddered beneath the hot, forceful passion of his kiss, desire and disgust battling inside her, and only dimly registered his words as he took his mouth from hers.

'You can't help yourself.' His silver eyes challenged her to deny him.

'Oh, but I can.' she shot back, and, shoving him hard in the chest, she continued, 'You can take yourself and your filthy proposition out of my apartment, and don't come back.' Swinging on her heel, she marched to the door.

'Wait, Beth. I have not finished.'

'Well, I have. In fact, I finished with you two weeks ago, and nothing has changed.'

'But situations do change, Beth.' He strolled towards where she stood at the door. 'Your stepbrother, for instance, he's gained a promotion, a much better salary and a fiancée, I believe, all in a couple of weeks.'

She stared up at him. Why had he changed the subject so quickly? Then, with a growing sense of dread, she listened to him.

'You see, Beth, the account I gave Brice Wine Merchants via Mike, the account that earned him his promotion, can just as easily be cancelled. Elizabeth is a lovely girl, but how will she feel when Mike's income is cut in half? Or he might even lose his job.'

'Are you threatening me?' she said, all the colour draining from her face, not wanting to believe what she was hearing.

'As if I would.' A ruthless smile curved his sensuous mouth. 'No, I am simply giving you a possible scenario... The rest is up to you. I will be at my usual hotel until ten tomorrow morning. I suggest you consider your options and give me a call before I leave.'

'That is blackmail, you bastard!' she cried, incensed that he would even try such a trick.

'Not at all. In the business world, that is a deal,' Dex

responded hardly, not in the least bothered by her outburst. 'Take it or leave it.' Withdrawing a pen from his inside pocket, he caught her hand in his.

Beth tried to pull her hand free, but with insulting ease he held it firm, palm up, and had the audacity to write on her soft flesh. Curling her fingers into a fist, he let her go.

'The number of my hotel and suite. Any time before ten in the morning, I will be available. You have until then to decide.'

'Why, you...' She couldn't think of a name foul enough, and swung out at him instead. But Dex caught her wrist in mid-air, and, grabbing her other hand with one large hand he encircled her slender wrists and pinned them back against the wall above her head. He stared down at her, rage contorting his features for a split second. Her heart jolted and she caught her breath.

Then he moved slowly, deliberately, his long body pressing her against the wall.

'I told you once before...' But he didn't finish. His steel-grey eyes raked down her body. His hand lifted and closed over her breast, kneading the firm flesh, his thumb finding the hardening nipple beneath the soft fabric, and she stifled a groan.

'All that fiery passion going to waste. How much more satisfying to channel it into the bedroom.' His hand slipped down and under her sweater, closing over her naked flesh. She knew he was doing it deliberately; he wanted to punish her. Still she groaned. She couldn't control or deny her surrender to the sweet torture of his touch.

'Remember this when you make your decision.' He watched her, his silver eyes burning through her.

Beth stared back, hopelessly disorientated. Then she recognised the glitter of masculine triumph in his eyes and burnt with shame and anger. 'Damn you!' she swore under her breath.

Dex abruptly let go of her hands and jerked back. 'Don't forget, before ten, Beth.' He opened the door and left.

didn't love Dex... and she didn't care...

CHAPTER EIGHT

MECHANICALLY Beth slipped the chain on the door and
shot the dead bolt. *Dead bolt.* How appropriate. She felt
half dead, and also like bolting.

Served her right, she thought guiltily. She had never
celebrated Hallowe'en before, never really wanted to,
probably because of her convent education. Look what
happened the first time she did. Dexter Giordanni! The
party had not really been her scene at all. Mike had
talked her into it. But to give him his due even he had
been quite shocked, and they had all left early.

Moving slowly, she made her way to the bedroom,
switching off the lights as she went, though she didn't
bother with the light in her bedroom. She slipped off her
green sweatsuit, and climbed into bed, her mind spinning
like a windmill. The magnitude of the night's events
were too horrible to contemplate, but she had to...

It would be laughable if it wasn't so scary. Dex
wanted her to be his—what? Girlfriend, mistress, lover?
The awful truth was she was tempted to agree. Dex
didn't love her, but that didn't stop her wanting him with
every fibre of her being. She tried to tell herself it was
just sex, but deep down she knew that for her it was
much, much more. She wanted to take anything Dex had
to offer—love or lust, she didn't care. She'd even agree
to blackmail!

With a low groan Beth rolled over on the bed and
buried her face in the pillow. She blushed with shame.

125

God help her. Had she no pride? No self-respect? Apparently not.

She had been fooling herself for the past two weeks, trying to pretend she didn't care. Telling herself she didn't love Dex, that it had been an indiscretion borne of inexperience, and thank God she'd found out the truth about him in time, before she'd got in too deep.

A bitter smile twisted her lovely mouth. Earlier this evening she had been congratulating herself on reviving her social life. Seeing Dex tonight had brought that idea to an abrupt end. When she had managed to swallow her anger she had enjoyed dancing with him, and the rest…his kisses, the feel of his strong hand on her flesh. Suddenly every pulse in her body responded at the memory, and, despising her own weakness she jumped out of bed.

She was too agitated to sleep anyway, and, slipping on her robe, she wandered back into the living room and clicked on the light. Her eye caught the ink on her hand. Staring at her palm, she traced the black numbers with the finger of her other hand. The man was seriously weird, she told herself as she paced the room back and forth, her mind in turmoil, too restless even to sit down.

Why? Why was Dex trying to force her into being his mistress? It didn't make sense. So, all right, he thought she was in competition for his sister's man. But surely a man of his intelligence must know enough about human relations to realise nothing would force Paul Morris into staying with his sister if he didn't want to. In fact Dex and Paul were very much alike: highly successful, wealthy, very eligible, and experienced enough to escape the clutches of any woman if they wanted to.

No. She was missing something. But what? The underlying bitterness, the anger she had sensed in Dex

tonight was directed at her. Maybe it was simply a male
ego thing. She had insulted Dex by jilting him two
weeks ago, and compounded her folly by telling him
tonight she would like to kill him. It was after that comment he had turned into a cold, hard-faced stranger.
Then he had threatened Beth with her stepbrother's
downfall unless she complied with Dex's demands.
Somehow it didn't ring true.

She thought back to the first time they had met, at the
Brice party. She had been bowled over from the minute
she clapped eyes on Dex, but even then her feminine
intuition had warned her to stay clear of him. But, un-
cannily like her mother, Beth had let her heart rule her
head. For a few short days she had been gloriously
happy, only to be plunged into the depths of despair
when she'd discovered Dex, the man she loved, was using her for his own ends.

Jilting him had been the hardest thing she had ever
done. Pride alone had seen her though the last two
weeks, and if she gave in to Dex's disgraceful proposition now, she would lose even that.

But what of her stepbrother, Mike? What might he
lose if she said no to Dex? Much as she adored Mike,
she would not sleep with a man for him. Then it hit
her—she could swallow her pride for Mike, and tell Dex
the truth. If she'd done that two weeks ago she might
not be in the mess she was in now.

The cold pale light of dawn was slanting through the
window when Beth finally reached her decision. A wry
smile tilted the corners of her mouth. It was so obvious
she should have realised straight away.

Once she told Dex the real reason she had jilted him—
she had overheard the conversation between Dex and his
friend Bob—and admitted that Paul Morris was her god-

father, he'd realize she was no threat to his sister. Any interest Dex had in her would vanish like a whistle in the wind, along with any need to harm Mike. Dex might even have the grace to feel ashamed of the way he had treated her. But she doubted it. He was ruthless in the pursuit of what he wanted, that much she had learnt from their brief relationship.

With her decision made, Beth went back to bed. She had time for a few hour's sleep before calling Dex at his hotel with the truth.

A long way off a bell was ringing. Beth stirred and half opened her eyes. The ringing stopped and she rolled over in bed and snuggled back down. She was so tired, and today was Saturday—no work, she thought contentedly.

Ringing! Her eyes flew wide open and she shot up in bed, the events of last night flashing through her mind. She turned her head, looked at the clock on the bedside table, and groaned. 'Oh, my God!' she exclaimed, and closed her eyes again for a second in disbelief.

She could not believe it. She had overslept. She opened her eyes again and looked once more at the clock. There was no mistake. Eleven in the morning. It could only happen to her! Still, she tried... Leaping out of bed and dashing into the kitchen, she picked up the telephone and studied the palm of her hand. Was that a three or an eight? The heat of her palm in her sleep had smudged the numbers.

Frantically Beth dialled what she hoped was the right number, and got a Mercedes car dealership! She tried again and heaved a sigh of relief when a female voice answered, announcing the name of Dex's hotel. Her relief quickly turned to horror when she was informed that Mr Giordanni had checked out not ten minutes ago and

was on his way to Heathrow to catch the Concorde flight
to New York.

Beth staggered into the living room, collapsed in the
armchair and groaned. Well, fate had taken a hand. That
was it. Dex had his answer by default. There was nothing
she could do about it now. She tried to cheer herself up
with the thought there was nothing Dex could do about
Mike, at least not for the next two days. But Monday
was a different matter.

Beth toyed with the idea of ringing Mike and telling
him what had happened, then decided against it. There
was no point in worrying her stepbrother unduly. It
crossed her mind to try and get in touch with Dex, and
then she realised he had never actually given her so
much as his address or home telephone number. She
didn't even know for certain where he lived. Rome or
New York, he had said. She could ring the Seymour
Club and ask how to get in touch with him, but did she
really want to?

No... Swallowing her pride for her stepbrother had
seemed a good idea last night. But Beth was a fatalist.
Why bother? Mike was good at his job, and he was old
enough and man enough to make it on his own. As for
Elizabeth, Beth had no doubt the girl would stand by
him whatever he did. It was real love she had seen between the pair of them last night. Not the shallow copy
Dex had pretended to feel for Beth.

All those out-of-the-way intimate restaurants Dex had
taken her to—she had thought they were romantic. With
the clarity of hindsight she realised his reasons had been
much more basic. He had never even once suggested she
accompany him to his hotel. Dex had obviously not
wanted their brief relationship or engagement made public. Because he had known from the start it was a fake.

Getting to her feet, Beth walked into the kitchen and made herself a cup of coffee. Sipping the reviving brew, she concluded it was probably as well it had ended this way. Dex could do his damnedest for all she cared. He no longer had any hold over her. He had broken her heart, but he would never know. She was young enough and strong enough to recover, she told herself. And if the thought echoed hollowly in the corner of her mind, there was no one to hear it but Beth.

She spent a miserable weekend, and could barely wait to get home on Monday evening and ring Mike. She quizzed him tactfully about work, but he was fine—his job was fine. Still Dex's threat preyed on her mind. As each day passed she found her nerves getting more and more strung out, waiting for the proverbial clog to drop...

Until she opened her mail on Friday evening. Curled up in the armchair, a glass of wine on the table in front of her, she read the letter again. It was a brief, cheerful note from her godfather, inviting her to stay with him at a villa on the Isle of Capri next weekend. He had already squared it with her boss, Cecil, and the air ticket was enclosed. She was to fly out the following Friday and stay until the Sunday. She was to bring her glad rags. He was getting married to 'the lady of the lamb noisettes,' he joked.

Beth dropped the letter and the ticket on the table, and, picking up the wine glass, took a large swallow. She needed it. Replacing the glass on the table, she grimaced. So that was it... Her worries were over.

Now she knew why Dex hadn't carried out his threat to ruin Mike. His sister had got her man. There was no need for Dex to pretend he wanted Beth. She was no danger any more. And obviously by now he must know Paul was her godfather.

A long drawn-out sigh escaped her. She supposed she should be relieved, but instead she simply felt sad. Her first thought was not to go to the wedding because she'd see Dex. But she knew Paul would be deeply hurt if she did not attend. Then, as she sat there sipping her wine, mulling over the way Dex had used her, she got angry. She was going to the wedding. It would be worth it just to show Dexter Giordanni she could be as sophisticated and blasé as he was, and if she embarrassed Dex by her presence all the better...

With a sense of growing excitement, Beth boarded the ferry boat that was taking her on the last part of her journey to Capri. The flight had been uneventful; a taxi driver with her name on a placard had met her at Naples Airport and delivered her to the ferry boat. It was a beautiful autumn afternoon. The sun shone from a clear blue sky and the temperature was a balmy sixty degrees. She had never been to Italy before, never mind to Capri, and she was really looking forward to it.

She stood at the prow of the boat, dressed in blue jeans, a green sweater and a jacket, her auburn hair blowing in the breeze. The island rose like a jewel from the clear blue sea. It was more rugged than she had imagined, but absolutely beautiful. Eagerly her eyes scanned the dockside as the ferry tied up in the small port, and, spying Paul's elegant figure standing on the jetty, she waved frantically.

In minutes she was in his arms, and with the greetings over he led her to a blue Mercedes car. Her glance darted all over. There was a funicular railway that took passengers up the sharply rising cliff, and the road Paul took wound very steeply in a corkscrew up the hillside, the sea never far from view. She looked back down on the bustle of the port, and Paul pointed out where the famous Blue Grotto was. Finally managing to contain her excitement, she looked at Paul.

'So, you're getting married. Are you sure?' she asked. She loved him, but she knew just how volatile the members of the Giordanni family could be. Her godfather was a lovely man, but very British.

Paul glanced at her, his pale eyes serious. 'Yes, Beth. I have never been more sure of anything in my life.'

'I'm happy for you,' she said sincerely, and she was. Then the car was sweeping around a sharp corner and into the concealed entrance of a narrow road that dipped steeply down again. Beth gasped. It felt as though they were driving into the sea.

'Impressive, hmm?'

'That is an understatement,' Beth whispered as the car swept through large iron gates on to a wide drive, to stop in front of a magnificent whitewashed villa that faced straight out to sea.

Half an hour later, Beth stood beside a huge four-poster bed and looked around in awe. An elderly house-keeper had unpacked and hung up her few clothes, and left. The bedroom was exquisite, a symphony in white and gold, with just a touch of blue in the marble mosaic floor. She crossed to where another door opened off the room, and gasped at the sheer size and elegance of the *en suite* bathroom. Whoever owned this place certainly knew how to live. She was almost afraid to use the facilities, but she did. After quickly washing her face and hands, she kept her jeans on but changed her sweater for a white polo top. It was so much warmer here than in London; she could not believe it.

Making her way back down the grandly curving staircase, she felt almost like Vivien Leigh in *Gone with the Wind*. Her lips twitched. Except for her jeans and shirt. Catching sight of Paul waiting for her in the huge reception hall, she flashed him a full-blown smile. 'This is some villa.'

'Yes, it is nice,' he said in his understated way. 'But what can I get you, Beth? A drink? Something to eat?'

'Can we go outside while it's still light? I'd love to see the gardens.'

'I suppose so. Anna won't be here for a couple of hours yet; so we have time.' With an indulgent smile he took her hand in his and led her out of the door and across the wide drive to a band of immaculately manicured grass.

'Oh, can we go down the steps?' Beth cried in delight, pulling on his hand. An ornate balustrade encircled the whole villa, intercepted by massive semi-circular steps that led down to a wide terrace, with a swimming pool to one side.

'Sometimes I forget you're grown up,' Paul said, stopping for a moment and smiling down into her excited green eyes. 'You have the same enthusiasm for life as your father had.'

Freeing her hand from his, she reached up and cupped his face, and kissed him lightly. 'Thank you.' She stepped back just as a car screeched to a halt in the drive.

Beth glanced across, her eyes widening incredulously as she saw Dex leap out of the car, dressed in black. His face equally black with fury, he charged towards them.

'You bastard, Morris,' he snarled, his lips drawn back against his teeth in savage, primitive rage. His fist shot out and thudded against Paul's face, sending him sprawling flat on his back on the grass.

It had all happened so quickly Beth couldn't believe it. The air crackled with violent tension, and she stood frozen in shock.

'And you...' Dex turned on Beth, murder in his eyes. 'You—you...' His English temporarily failed him and he let go in a torrent of Italian as he grabbed her around the waist and dragged her towards the open door of the car. 'You're out of here.' His breathing ragged, he bundled her into the car, slid into the driver's seat and gunned the engine.

Beth grabbed the door handle, but it was locked. She glanced frantically out of the window, her horrified eyes catching sight of a dazed Paul trying to sit up. Then, in a death-defying turn, Dex spun the car around. Beth fell heavily against him, her hand grabbing his thigh. He jerked his leg away and shot her a vitriolic glance.

She struggled to sit up and fell back against the door of the passenger seat, as far away from him as she could get. She was terrified. She had never seen such speed before in her life. By the time she caught her breath Dex had the car off the drive and racing up the perilously narrow road.

'Slow down! You'll kill us!' she cried, her voice hoarse with fear.

'If it keeps you away from him,' he grated through clenched teeth, 'I will.' Dex glanced at her, his expression murderous.

'You're mad. Totally mad,' she cried as they hit what passed for the main road at what felt like the speed of light. The car skidded and Beth closed her eyes and prayed.

'You can open your eyes,' he spat. 'I am not going to kill myself for a whore like you.'

Beth felt the car slow down and she opened her eyes.

She shot a fearful look at Dex's granite-like profile. A muscle jerked in his cheek and his mouth was a tight line of rage. She could sense the violence radiating from him, and she hardly dared breathe. She dropped her eyes to where his long fingers curved around the steering wheel, his knuckles white with the pressure of his grip.

She didn't dare speak; she was too frightened he would drive them off the road. She tensed as a moment later he did drive off the road, swinging onto a cart track that led through a small copse of trees and stopping dead a few feet from the edge of a cliff. But it didn't make Beth feel any better.

Dex turned in his seat and watched her for a long moment. 'Nothing to say?' he demanded harshly. 'No whimpering feminine excuse?'

'Let me out of this car,' she whispered.

'The door is open.'

Grasping the handle, Beth opened the door and tumbled out of the car onto the ground. She crawled on her hand and knees, her breath coming in great gasps until she was well away from the car and its crazy driver. Then she sat down, drawing her knees up to her chest and resting her head on them.

She was trembling with shock. She bit her lip to stop herself crying and thanked the Lord for the hard ground beneath her. For a moment in the car she had really feared for her life.

'Tears won't wash away your sins, and they certainly have no effect on me.' Dex's harsh voice broke the silence, and reluctantly Beth lifted her head.

He was standing in front of her, dressed all in black—black jeans and a black sweater—his legs slightly apart and his hands clenching and unclenching at his sides. He looked like some dark avenging angel.

'I am not crying,' she managed to say, with a slight tremor in her voice. 'I am simply in shock. I have never been kidnapped by a madman before.' She was beginning to regain some self-control, and she was also beginning to get angry.

'You call me mad? *Dio*, woman, how could you? Have you no pride? No self-respect?' Dex demanded, his voice crackling with fury.

His words beat down on her like so many stones of wrath. She slid back and stood up, making sure she kept well away from him. She could feel the menace in him, and even as it frightened her it made her temper rise.

'You trek halfway across Europe after a man who is getting married tomorrow—a man who does not love you and is old enough to be your father!' he shouted, stepping towards her.

Fear made Beth step back, and she gasped, suddenly realising Dex didn't know the truth about her and Paul. 'He is my *god*father,' she emphasised, and shivered as his hard face convulsed with rage.

'Tell that to the marines,' he snarled. 'I know the Morrises of this world. They don't befriend innocent little virgins for nothing. And you thought I wasn't good enough for you. What a joke,' he drawled derisively.

Beth's face turned red, and then white with anger. 'I don't give a damn what you think.' Her green eyes blazed in the paleness of her face. 'Paul *is* my godfather and he *does* love me—always has, from the day I was born.' She registered the shock in Dex's grey eyes and relished in it. 'And I trekked "halfway across Europe", as you so nicely put it, because Paul asked me to be at his wedding. Now, what is your excuse,' she demanded furiously, 'for knocking out a perfectly innocent man?

You great bully!' She hurled the accusation at him, her green eyes, full of contempt, clashing with his.

Dex spun around, stalked back to the car and slammed the passenger door shut as if he wanted to knock it off its hinges. *Cristo*! He swore long and furiously in a vicious spate of Italian. Then, as Beth watched, he squared his shoulders, tension in every line of his long body, and turned back to face her.

His face a rigid mask, he stepped forward. 'If Morris is your godfather,' he grated in a chillingly quiet voice, 'then why did you not tell me?'

The great Dexter Giordanni had finally made a mistake, Beth realised, her anger subsiding. Finally the moment of truth. Revenge was sweet and she was going to enjoy every second of it.

'You never asked me.' She looked straight up into his dark face. 'In fact, if memory serves me right, we met Paul once in your casino and you never mentioned him again.' Get out of that one, you lying swine, she thought, but didn't say, and almost grinned at the host of conflicting emotions that warred in his steely grey eyes—not least confusion.

'Nothing to say, Dex?' she prompted. The phrase 'hoist by his own petard' sprang to mind.

Dex's head bent and he stared fixedly at the ground for a long moment. The silence stretched, fraught with simmering emotion. Then slowly Dex lifted his head again. He didn't look at her; his eyes avoided hers. His tanned face was a blank mask, but a muscle beating wildly in his cheek betrayed his agitation.

'You're right. I didn't ask you about Morris. I didn't ask because I was violently jealous.' His gaze flicked to hers and Beth was almost fooled by the glint of naked anguish in his eyes, 'Today when I saw you kissing

Morris I saw red. It was unforgivable of me to hit him, but you know how I feel about you. How much I want you. I am a jealous, possessive man. I can't help it where you're concerned.'

He took another step towards her, and Beth moved back.

'You're also a lying hound where I am concerned,' she said coldly. 'And have been from the moment we met. So save your play-acting for someone who might appreciate it.' She was disgusted. Even now Dex was not going to admit the truth, and she had had enough.

He watched her, his grey eyes narrowing intently on her small face, then he said curtly, 'I am not acting. Why do you think that?'

Beth looked past him to the edge of the cliff, the deep blue of the sea beyond, and on to the far horizon where the sun was sinking in a red blaze of glory. Her dream of love and happy-ever-after had sunk in very much the same way. Drowned in a red blaze of passion. She tilted her head back and looked up into Dex's face. And it was all his fault.

'Because, Dex, I know everything. I know why you took me out in the first place. You asked me out to keep me away from Paul, the man your sister wanted.'

'No...' he denied angrily, reaching out and grabbing her by the shoulders. 'It wasn't like that.'

'Don't bother to deny it, Dex, I heard you say it.' His hands tightened on her flesh, but she didn't care. Beth wasn't frightened any more; she simply wanted the whole sorry mess over and done with.

'When? Where?' he asked, his body rigid.

'The day you came back from New York. The day I called at the Seymour.'

'The day you jilted me,' he cut in, his dark brows drawn together in a frown, his grey eyes searching hers.

'Yes. I didn't leave a note. I didn't visit a sick friend. But I did sit in the outer office at the club. The intercom was on.' She wasn't going to tell him she had switched it on. 'And I heard you discuss in some detail your ex-wife—someone you conveniently forgot to mention to me—your so-called fiancée.'

His hands fell from her shoulders and he drew himself up to his full height. All the colour drained from his face, leaving him grey beneath his tan.

'You were laughing with your friend. Bob, I think?' She arched one delicate brow enquiringly.

'Bob.' He cursed under his breath, and Beth knew he was remembering.

'Yes, you were having a drink with him. You had plenty of time—the girl would wait. You told him you were engaged, but not necessarily getting married, and you also told him why. The girl was going out with your sister's man, and you saw a way to put a stop to it. Fate gave you the opportunity in the guise of Brice Wine Merchants party. Need I go on? Or can you put the rest together yourself?' she taunted him.

'I remember the conversation.' A dark red stain swept up his face. At least he had the grace to blush, Beth thought bitterly. 'And I know how it must have sounded, but—'

'Don't bother explaining.' Beth stopped him, raising her hand. 'I'm not a fool. Your only reason for seeing me was your sister. You recognised me as the girl dining with Paul when your sister threw his dinner over him. You used me, and you were still trying to use me two weeks ago. You even tried to blackmail me.' She laughed, a harsh sound in the silence. 'I spent a week worrying about Mike—until I got the wedding invitation and realised your problem was solved.'

He winced, but responded curtly, 'Not quite. No one told me about Morris. If you had been honest and told me the real reason for jilting me, the rest need never have happened.'

Lifting her chin, Beth stared straight into his eyes. 'Oh, so now it's my fault?' She shook her head, her auburn hair flowing around her face. 'If you had let me finish speaking when we met Paul at the club, instead of dashing us away and kissing me senseless...' Beth didn't want to remember their lovemaking and stopped. What was the use of arguing with Dex?

'You're incredible.' Beth shook her head sadly. 'You do exactly what you want, take exactly what you want, and never once question how anyone else feels. You disgust me.'

She had gone too far. Dex caught her wrist and twisted it around her back, bringing her flush against his hard body. 'Disgust you?' he said, with deadly coldness. 'It wasn't disgust but pure lust you felt in my arms in your bed. And I can prove it,' he grated harshly.

Beth stared at him, her anger dying fast as his grey gaze roamed insolently over her. She saw the hunger in his eyes as his dark head lowered. She raised a hand to ward him off, but he simply hauled her tighter to him, her hand pressed to his chest. Wildly she shook her head. 'Don't!' she gasped.

But Dex merely laughed. 'Why not? I have nothing to lose.' His other hand gently caught her long hair and wrapped it around his wrist. His mouth poised above hers, Dex watched her ruthlessly. 'You've made a fool of me and you're going to pay.'

Beth shivered, her tongue slipping out to moisten suddenly dry lips. He had her trapped. She moved her head back with a jerk as his mouth ground down on hers and he began kissing her with a savage, urgent passion. She tried to prevent her lips parting in response, her body from arching against his, but desire sharp as a knife flared up inside her, and helplessly she found herself responding.

Her lips moved under his as she kissed him back. She was beyond thinking sensibly any more. His hand stroked down to curve over her bottom and pull her hard against his thighs. A moan escaped her and she trembled at the evidence of his masculine arousal pressed against her soft female mound. She heard his swift intake of breath as her hips moved involuntarily against him, and rejoiced in the knowledge of how she affected him.

When he thrust her away from him she almost fell. A steadying hand on her shoulder kept her upright, but his touch was hard and impersonal.

'We have to go back—I to apologise to your godfather and you to gloat.'

She glanced up at his hard face and knew he was as disgusted with himself as she was.

CHAPTER NINE

DEX held open the car door and gestured for her to get in.

Beth hesitated. Dex was wrong. She had no desire to gloat. Instead she felt an overwhelming sadness for what she had lost.

He mistook her hesitation for fear. 'You have nothing to be afraid of, Beth. I wouldn't deliberately harm a hair of your head. Now get in. I promise I will not drive fast.'

The journey back to the villa was short and completed in absolute silence. Until Dex turned the car into the drive and saw another car parked in front of the entrance.

'*Dio!*' Dex groaned, and for a second rested his head on the steering wheel.

Beth glanced at him and for a moment felt some sympathy for him, but then she saw again Dex lashing out at the unsuspecting Paul, and she checked herself in time. He did not deserve her sympathy. Opening the door, she jumped out of the car and started towards the house.

Suddenly a woman came flying out, a woman Beth immediately recognised as Dex's sister, and she looked just as excitable as the only other time Beth had seen her. She shot past Beth and yelled at Dex.

Beth looked back in amazement as Dex stood granite-faced while his sister Anna bawled him out. She jumped when a hand fell on her shoulder. Turning around, she looked up into the familiar face of Paul.

'Are you all right, Bethany?' he asked quietly. The beginning of a magnificent black eye was marring his handsome features. 'In the excitement of the past few weeks, I forgot I saw you with Dexter at the casino until he dragged you off today. I was worried about you. Is there something going on between you two I don't know about?'

'No, of course not. I met him with Mike and he offered to show me his new casino—full stop.' Beth couldn't tell Paul the truth. 'And you have no need to worry, I'm fi—' That was as far as she got, before Paul cut across her.

'What the hell did you think you were playing at, Giordanni? Aiming a punch at me I can understand—maybe I deserved it—but dragging off my goddaughter...'

Beth spun around to find Dex standing stiffly behind her. One look at his dark face and she knew he had overheard her conversation with Paul. But he looked straight over the top of her head at Paul, his face a grim mask. Anna moved to link her arm through Paul's while smiling rather shamefacedly at Beth.

'Paul,' Dex said curtly, acknowledging the other man's outburst before continuing, 'I thought I was protecting my sister's honour. But nothing I say can possibly excuse my disgraceful actions. I apologise from the bottom of my heart. I should not have lashed out at you. I am deeply sorry and ashamed. I can only beg your forgiveness and hope in time you can forget my appalling behaviour. I have already apologised to my sister, and of course to Bethany.'

Beth slanted a glance at him from beneath her thick lashes. As apologies went it was a sizzler, and there was no mistaking the sincerity in Dex's dark eyes. But she did not remember him apologising to her, she thought mutinously. She was about to say so when Anna held out her hand towards her, and, nudging Paul, said, 'Please introduce me.'

The introductions made, Anna bent to kiss Beth's cheek. By the time the social niceties were completed, they were walking into the drawing room.

Beth hesitated, slightly overawed by the opulence of her surroundings. 'This is a wonderful house.' She turned to Paul. 'Have you rented it or what?' she asked, more for something to say than anything else. There was still tension in the air, undercurrents she did not understand.

'Good heavens, no.' Paul chuckled and led her to a cream silk-covered sofa, one of a pair, placed at either side of a massive marble fireplace. 'Dexter owns the villa, though according to Anna he's rarely here. Anna works and lives in Naples. That's where we met. Anna decided to get married from here because there's more room to accommodate the few close friends who are attending the wedding. At my age, and in the circumstances, a big wedding would be out of place.'

Dex really had been secretive with her, Beth thought. Not once had he mentioned a home in Capri. It only confirmed what she already knew: he didn't give a damn about her. But if she had known it was Dex's villa Paul had invited her to stay in, she would never have come— much as she loved her godfather. She didn't want to be beholden to Dex in any way whatsoever.

Dinner was served in a huge formal dining room, and was fraught to say the least! Beth ached to escape to her room. Revenge was not sweet, she realised, sitting at the table, eating the exquisitely prepared food and waited on by a houseboy wearing white gloves! She might not understand Italian, but it was pretty obvious Anna had not forgiven Dex for assaulting her fiancé.

Paul explained the arrangements for the simple wedding service the next day, but after that it was heavy going. Paul's eye had turned purple, and as far as Beth could gather Dex was being blamed for ruining tomorrow's wedding before it had even taken place.

As for Dex, he barely said a word. Beth found her attention drawn to him over and over again. He sat at the head of the great table, wearing a black formal evening suit and brilliant white shirt, his handsome features set in a hard mask of iron control. He looked even more dangerously formidable than usual. The few times he caught her glance, he stared at her so coldly she quickly looked away, afraid the others would notice.

She heaved a sigh of relief when the meal ended and coffee was served in the drawing room. She sat down on the sofa and gratefully took the cup of coffee the houseboy handed her.

'We did not meet in the best way,' Anna said, sitting down beside Beth. 'I am sorry, but Paul—we fight, I see you... I do not know...'

'I was his goddaughter.' Beth helped Anna out with her halting English. 'It's all right, we laughed about it afterwards, and I am very happy for you both.'

'Thank you. I wish to be friends.' They smiled a smile of mutual understanding. 'I also apologise for my brother. He thinks he protects my honour. He thinks Paul has betrayed me. He sees him kiss you and goes *pazzo*.'

Whatever *pazzo* meant, Beth was pretty sure she did not want to discuss it.

'Beth does not understand, Anna, and she looks tired.' Dex appeared at the side of the sofa, his narrowed gaze concentrated on his sister, and he said something quickly in Italian before looking down on Beth. 'Come, I will show you to your room.'

Her green eyes clashed angrily with cool grey. Cheeky swine! she thought. More or less saying she looked a wreck. And whose fault was that? 'I can find my own way.' Beth jumped to her feet. Dex's height was intimidating.

'After my disgraceful behaviour earlier, please allow me to redeem myself by acting as a good host,' Dex drawled smoothly.

She wanted to object, but he made it sound so reasonable. Was she the only one to recognise the cynicism in his tone? She looked around for Paul but he had joined Anna on the sofa, and unless she wanted to make a scene in front of the happy couple there was nothing to do but agree. She said her goodnights, and, not looking at Dex, walked out of the room.

Once in the hall Beth dashed for the stairs, but Dex, with his long legs, was at her side in a second.

'You can drop the good host act,' Beth said tersely, ascending the stairs, very aware of his long-limbed body matching her step by step. 'I know the way, thank you very much,' she told him, trying to ignore the way her heart pounded too fast as he shadowed her so closely, and vainly trying to convince herself it was the exertion of climbing the stairs.

His hand gripped her shoulder as she reached the landing and turned to go right. 'Not so fast, Beth, we need to talk.'

Beth was wearing her one and only formal dress, the slip of black and gold satin. She felt the searing imprint of his fingers on her naked flesh, and trembled inside. She shrugged, trying to shake him off. Looking up at his harshly handsome face, she gave him a tight-lipped smile, refusing to let him see how much he disturbed her.

'No, I think not,' she responded distantly. 'We are guests at a wedding, nothing more. Let's just leave it at that.' And, turning on her heel, she'd actually made it to her bedroom door when Dex's voice stopped her.

'Good, so you have no objection to my telling Paul the truth about the relationship between you and I? That is a relief,' he drawled sardonically.

Beth, in the act of opening the door, spun around. 'What?' she looked up, meeting his eyes with horror.

Dex was standing a foot away, his eyes narrowed speculatively on her flushed face. 'Lying even by omission can get a person into a heap of trouble, I always thought. Don't you agree?' he asked, in a voice laced with sarcasm.

Beth knew he was referring to her, and she had a feeling it would be a long time before he forgot she had lied to him. Nervously she backed into the bedroom. He followed her inside without waiting for an invitation, and closed the door firmly behind him. Switching on the light, he looked at Beth, and she almost stumbled under the sheer intensity of his gaze.

'I only want to talk,' Dex said, with the tilt of one dark brow. 'Not leap on you.'

'All right,' she breathed, but spun on her heel and crossed the room to the window. She needed the time to gather her wits, and, swallowing hard, she turned slowly around to face him.

He stared across the room at her. 'Is this bedroom all right for you?'

The mundane question came as a surprise. Beth glanced around the luxuriously appointed bedroom, her glance lingering on the lovely four-poster bed with the elegant floating drapes. 'It's fine,' she said. 'A vast improvement on mine at home.'

Seeing the direction of her gaze, Dex drawled, 'Oh, I don't know. I have very fond memories of your bed.'

Her head jerked back and she looked at him, a vivid image of his large naked body, limbs entwined with her own, flashing in her mind's eye. Her green eyes widened warily on his dark face. She didn't trust him an inch, and she was none too sure about herself. Suddenly the intimacy of the situation hit her. She shivered, and nervously smoothed the skirt of her dress down over her hips with damp palms.

Dex shook his black head and smiled grimly. 'Don't panic. I said talk, and that is what I meant.' He moved a few steps towards her and then stopped, and Beth had the weirdest notion that he was also nervous.

'So?' she prompted softly.

'I owe you an apology. You were right. I did ask you out because I thought you were going out with Paul Morris, and I did do it for my sister. Under the circumstances I would probably do it again.'

Beth finally had her apology, back-handed though it was. She should have been pleased. But knowing the truth and having it spelt out were two different things, she realised sadly. It was no surprise, she tried to console herself, but instead all she felt was simmering pain and anger. 'You really are despicable. I think I hate you,' she said flatly.

'Hate me as much as you like, but let me finish.' Dex raked a hand through his hair in a frustrated gesture, then hesitated for a moment. 'I overheard you telling Paul you and I dated once. End of story. I take it you do not want your godfather or my sister to know the truth?'

'You've got that right,' she muttered, wondering why

the abrupt change of subject but accepting it. 'For some bizarre reason Paul thinks you were entitled to swing a punch at him, so why disillusion him?' Her eyes met his. 'And I'm sure it's what you want as well,' she gibed. 'I can still remember all the out-of-the-way places you took me to. To avoid being seen with me,' she said, bitterness making her voice harsh.

His grey eyes flared briefly, then the heavy lids narrowed, hiding his expression from her. 'Believe what you like, Beth. I am not going to argue with you. I am not trying to make excuses for my behaviour, it was inexcusable, but I want to try and explain.

'I told you once I was illegitimate. In my mother's circumstances it was considered the worst form of shame. Anna is my older sister. I was born eighteen months after my mother was widowed. Here in southern Italy a young, innocent girl making a mistake might eventually have been forgiven, but it wasn't very likely. For a newly widowed lady to have had a child was thought heinous. Even today, in the nineties, a lot of older women still wear black for the rest of their lives after the death of their husband.'

Beth's soft heart squeezed. 'You don't have—'

'I do. I want to,' Dex cut in. 'We lived in a little cottage down at the port. Here on Capri everyone knew of the circumstances of my birth. My mother braved it out for years, until I had made enough money and moved her to Naples.' Dex stared past her as if he was in a world of his own, remembering. 'My mother died two years ago a very bitter woman, still not forgiven by the friends of her youth.'

'Why are you telling me all this?' Beth asked quietly. Her eyes roamed over his darkly attractive face, the rumpled black wavy hair falling on his proud brow, and she could easily imagine him as a young boy, an outcast and vulnerable.

Dex moved closer to her and watched her through narrow intent eyes. 'Because I want you to understand why I behaved as I did. I am breaking a confidence in telling you, but I think you need to know. The reason Paul expected me to hit him is quite simple. He is an honourable man. He understands our Latin code of honour. Anna is pregnant, but not yet married. As her brother, I am entitled to knock the man out,' he declared emphatically.

Beth heard the underlying thread of violence in his tone and winced, but as for the rest she was pleased as punch. 'Pregnant,' she murmured. 'That's marvellous.' She smiled, a beaming grin. 'Paul will make a wonderful father, I know.' She was genuinely delighted.

'Now, yes! But about three months ago Paul and Anna parted. I do not usually involve myself with my sister's affairs, but this time was different. She later came to London to see Paul. She called his housekeeper, who told her where he was eating, and she dragged me along with her.'

Beth knew he was telling her the truth, she had overheard him saying as much, but unthinkingly she confirmed his words. 'That's how I always contact Paul, via Mrs Bewick. She always knows where he is.'

'Yes, well, on this occasion perhaps it would have been better if she had not. I saw you in the restaurant long before Anna did. A beautiful young girl smiling so lovingly at a much older man is always worthy of note. So often money is the incentive,' he drawled derisively.

His natural cynicism surfaced for a moment, and Beth felt a stab of distaste. At least now she could understand his reasoning a bit better, but it did not excuse Dex using her for his own ends. Nothing he said or did could repair the damage he had done to Beth, both mentally and physically.

'The rest, as you say, is history. Anna went crazy, and I got her out of the restaurant. Later, when I saw you again, I thought, why not me instead of Morris? I know what it is to be a bastard, and anything I can do to make sure Anna's child does not suffer the same fate I will do willingly,' Dex declared bluntly, his gaze skimming over her, lingering on the proud thrust of her breasts against the soft fabric of her dress, then moving with a flick of his lashes back to her face.

'And you are a very beautiful woman, Beth. It was no hardship.'

No hardship! Her body froze as the full meaning of his words sank in. 'You swine.' She looked up sharply and was shocked at the sensual light in his eyes. 'You...you arrogant creep,' she spluttered. She had almost felt sorry for him, imagining him as a young boy, the other children calling him names. Vulnerable? He was about as vulnerable as a rattlesnake, and twice as deadly.

He smiled, and, reaching out, he ran one long finger down the side of her face.

'Now that is what I wanted to talk about, Beth. Your temper and your obvious aversion to me. We are agreed no one will know of our brief fling. We are casual acquaintances—no more. But if you continue to look daggers at me, as you did tonight at dinner, and flinch every time I come near you, Paul and Anna might get suspicious. So we need a truce between us for the next two days.'

'We need a continent between us,' she prompted bitterly. 'But until I get off this island on Sunday you can have your truce. I don't want to upset Paul and Anna's wedding any more than it already has been.'

Dex eyed her consideringly. 'You mean that, Beth? Friends for the duration, hmm?'

'Yes.' She tilted her head back and boldly faced him. It would kill her, but she would try for Paul.

His hand reached out, catching her wrist. 'Shake on it,' he murmured, looking down into her upturned face. Their eyes met and held. 'Or maybe kiss on it.'

Beth's heart skipped a beat at the look in his eyes, but common sense prevailed. 'Don't push your luck, buster... Leave.'

He chuckled under his breath and, lifting her hand to his mouth, pressed a kiss on her knuckles. 'Thank you. Tomorrow is going to be hell. Paul barely tolerates me, and Anna has told me several times I have ruined their wedding day. The wedding photograph they keep for their children and their children's children will always show the bridegroom with a black eye.'

'Serves you right,' Beth said bluntly. 'It might teach you not to manipulate everyone you meet.' Beth spoke with more force than she realised, but she could still feel the disturbing warmth of his lips on her hand, and she resented her own weakness.

Abruptly Dex dropped her hand. His face darkened. 'I realise I might seem that way, but let me remind you, Beth,' he prompted, an odd harshness in his voice, 'it didn't work with you. You never called.'

Beth stared at him dumbly. What was he talking about? 'Ah, Mike,' she exclaimed. 'You mean your little attempt at blackmail? Sorry, I overslept.' She told him the truth without thinking.

He chuckled mirthlessly. 'You overslept.' Shaking his head, he gave her a cool smile. 'No matter, Beth.

Tomorrow we will behave as friends. Goodnight.'
Spinning on his heel, he left, closing the door quietly
behind him.

Beth was tired and tormented, and all she wanted to
do was shower and crawl into bed. Ten minutes later,
her toilet completed and wearing a short white nightie,
she climbed into the four-poster bed. Drawing the drapes
around the frame, she snuggled down under the covers.
The rest of the world was shut out.

But it was not so easy to shut off her troubled
thoughts. She was dreading tomorrow—the whole weekend! To pretend she was just a friend of Dex without
putting her foot in it was well beyond her acting capa-
bilities, she feared. Her godfather Paul was an astute
man; he knew her better than anyone. Still, she thought
hopefully, Paul had a lot more to worry about than Beth.
His new bride—the ceremony—his black eye!

Beth groaned and buried her head in the pillow. In
her mind's eye she saw Dex's handsome face contorted
by rage, and poor Paul laid out on the ground. In a way
it was partly her fault. If she had refused the wedding
invitation it would never have happened. But then again
Dex was a very Latin male. He saw himself as the pro-
tector of the females in his family. Hadn't he just told
her quite emphatically he felt entitled to slug Paul to
uphold the honour of his sister? Whether he thought
Beth was a threat to his sister or not. The truth was
probably somewhere in between, and on that disturbing
thought she finally fell into a restless sleep.

The small church decked out in flowers and ribbons was
the perfect setting for a perfect wedding. Beth sighed,
her green eyes misty, and brushed a tear from her cheek.
Anna, looking stunningly beautiful in a cream silk suit

overlaid with lace, and wearing a matching wide-brimmed hat with a short veil over her eyes, made her responses clear and true, as did Paul.

Suddenly a large hand holding a white hanky appeared in front of Beth. She glanced sideways at Dex, and took the hanky. 'Thank you,' she murmured. He looked incredibly sleek and handsome in a silver-grey three-piece suit that exactly matched his eyes, and she hastily looked away and dabbed at her moist eyes.

'Emotional little thing, aren't you?' Dex murmured, while staring straight ahead.

'Better than being a heartless swine,' Beth murmured under her breath. Her head bent as she folded the hanky into a perfect square and thrust it back at him without comment.

Dex pressed his large hand over hers. 'Time to leave, I think.'

Sure enough, the bride and groom were halfway down the aisle on their way out, followed by the best man, to whom Paul had introduced Beth earlier as the manager of his Italian estate. Beth frowned, remembering the rest of the conversation. Paul had also informed her that Dex was to take care of Beth for the wedding ceremony and the rest of the weekend. Which was why she had ended up stuck next to Dex in the front pew of the church.

Dex stood up, still holding Beth's hand, urged her to her feet and escorted her down the aisle. But as soon as they got outside Beth dodged behind the main wedding party and tried to lose herself in the crowd. If this was a small Italian wedding, she thought ruefully, sidling along the side of the church, hoping to escape attention, then heaven knew what a large wedding was like. It seemed to her everyone on the island had turned out. Not to mention the shock she had received earlier.

She had awoken to a house full of caterers, managing to grab a bite to eat in the kitchen and a cup of coffee before making herself scarce by exploring the terraced gardens. To her surprise, the terraces led right down to the sea and a private mooring. There, a sleek yacht had been tying up, with a couple of dozen very elegant people on board. Not wanting to be seen, she had hidden behind a large bush and watched as Dex appeared, already dressed formally for the wedding, and greeted the guests. Beth had dashed back to the house and was frantically getting ready when Paul had walked into the room. She'd mentioned the boat to him. Apparently the guests had been accommodated in a luxury hotel in Sorrento for the night, prior to attending the wedding.

'Hello, lady in red.'

Lost in thought, Beth jumped and turned her head. A ginger-haired man of about forty, with an open freckled face, smiled down at her. She recognised his voice immediately; it was indelibly printed on her brain.

'I'm Bob, and red is my colour—as you can see. Put me out of my misery and tell me your name,' he demanded, his blue eyes lit with amusement and a very masculine interest.

Beth grinned. She couldn't help it; there was something boyishly appealing about him. 'Bethany.' She offered her small hand.

'No rings,' Bob murmured, turning her hand over and lifting it to his lips. 'Better and better. I missed the wedding, but I have a feeling I am really going to enjoy the reception.' Beth chuckled. He was the most outrageous flirt.

'Bob. Where the hell were you?' Dex's hard voice interrupted the harmless banter.

Beth's hand was dropped like a hot potato and Bob's

blue eyes flicked assessingly from Dex to Beth and back to Dex again. 'The flight from New York was delayed—everything backed up. Sorry I missed the wedding.'

'I'll see you later,' Dex said curtly, and, turning his back on Bob, let his steely gaze fall on Beth. 'Paul wants you in the family photograph,' he said, and, slipping a long arm over her shoulders, turned her back towards the wedding group.

'All right. You don't have to drag me,' Beth snapped, resenting his arm around her, and resenting even more the way it made her feel.

His fingers tightened on her shoulder and his dark head inclined towards hers. 'A word of warning.' His breath brushed against her cheek, and she tensed. 'Don't waste your feminine wiles on Bob. He is far too smart to get caught.'

Beth gritted her teeth, ignoring his deliberate insult. 'Truce, remember?' she said, looking up into his unsmiling face.

'I remember. And I remember the first time I saw you in that suit.' His grey eyes raked down over her body, bringing a blush to her cheeks. 'You wore it today deliberately to get at me. I am not a fool Beth, so don't take me for one,' he drawled hardily.

'Dexter, *caro*.' The bridesmaid, a tall, elegant dark-haired girl, a friend of Anna, called to him, and Beth was spared from replying as Dex let her go and walked over to the girl.

Beth drew a ragged breath and smoothed the short skirt of her red suit down over her hips. She had vowed not to wear it again after the first time, when Dex had stripped it off her. But she was a realist. She had spent a fortune on the suit a month ago, and she had nothing else remotely suitable for an autumn wedding, and no money to buy anything new. But having Dex remind her was more than she could bear, and she felt the prick of tears behind her eyes—tears of self-pity, she knew.

But then Paul reached out to her and pulled her to his side. 'Come on, Beth, I need you to detract from my black eye.'

Forcing a smile to her flushed face, Beth wished the happy couple good luck. Then quickly the official photographer arranged the group. The photographs were taken amidst what Beth surmised were a lot of ribald comments on how the groom had got his black eye.

She tried to slip back into the crowd when the photographer had finished, but again she was foiled.

'You're coming in the car with me,' Dex said, taking her elbow and urging her to the waiting line of cars.

It got no better when they reached the villa. Paul and Anna greeted all the guests in the grand hall, and an elegant major-domo led everyone to the tables set out in the magnificent dining room. Beth was at the head table.

The caterers had been busy since the crack of dawn, and it was a typical Italian meal that went on for hours and hours. The food was excellent, but Beth tasted very little of it. She felt as if she was on display, and with Dex once again seated next to her she was intensely aware of every move he made. The champagne flowed like water, the talk was loud and happy—not that Beth understood it—and Dex played his part to perfection. He included her in the conversation by offering instant translations, he smiled and was unfailingly polite. But only she could see the ice in his eyes when he spoke to her.

Finally the best man stood up to speak and Beth breathed an audible sigh of relief. It can't be much longer now, she thought.

Dex bent his dark head towards her. 'Your boredom is showing, Beth.' His grey eyes glinted mockingly into hers. 'Weddings not your scene?'

With a flash of insight she realised Dex was right. 'No, not really. After attending three of my mother's, they tend to lose their appeal,' she responded coolly.

'I'm sorry.' He smiled softly, and she saw a glint of something very like pity in his eyes.

'Don't be.' She didn't need his sympathy; she didn't need anything from Dex. 'I'm not. But I suppose it's different for you. This must remind you of your own wedding, no doubt. Bring back pleasant memories, does it?' she goaded. As a conversation-stopper it was perfect.

The slight smile vanished from his face to be replaced with a hard mask of indifference. 'No.' Dex picked up his wine glass from the table, drained it, and ignored Beth for the rest of the reception.

By ten in the evening Beth had had more than enough. There were people everywhere. A trio was playing dance music and the huge hall had become the dance floor. She had danced with a dozen different men, drunk a few classes of champagne and was feeling absolutely shattered. Paul and Anna had left hours ago, for a destination unknown.

Beth sighed. She was in a room full of people and had never felt so alone. Paul, the one constant in her life, was married, and very soon would have his own family—which was only right. But Beth couldn't help the tears that welled up in her throat. Things would never be the same again.

Beth was considering her chances of slipping off to bed when a voice in her ear whispered, 'Our tune—care to dance?'

'Bob.' She grinned as she realised the band was playing 'Lady in Red'. 'Very funny,' she said—at least he spoke her language. 'But, no, thanks. I'm too hot.' She didn't dare take her jacket off, knowing the brevity of the camisole underneath.

'Okay. I'm not much of a dancer anyway. So, how about a stroll outside?'

Why not? she thought, and, linking her arm through his, she followed him outside and down onto the lower terrace, where the floodlit swimming pool gleamed in the darkness.

'Fresh air at last,' she murmured, taking a few deep breaths of the cool night air.

'Here, sit down, Beth, and relax.' Bob indicated a small patio table surrounded by chairs and pulled one out for her. Beth gratefully sat down.

'This is much better,' she said as Bob sat down in the chair opposite.

'Some party.' Bob smiled. 'But Dex doesn't look too happy in there.'

'Maybe the food didn't agree with him,' she said lightly, and grinned back at Bob. He was a nice, uncomplicated man, and she needed someone to take her mind off how very alone in the world she felt.

'The food of love, maybe,' Bob said seriously. 'I know who you are, Beth, and I know you and Dex were engaged.'

Beth felt the colour rise in her cheeks. 'It was a mistake.'

'I don't think so. I've seen the way he looks at you; he has hardly taken his eyes off you all evening. That's not like Dex. I've known him for years and I have never seen him show the least interest in a woman.'

'Please, I don't want to talk about him.'

'Don't be too hard on him, Beth. His ex-wife did a

real number on him. He was just starting out when they married, and he worked like a slave while she spent like a queen! Eventually she took off with a very rich, very much older man.'

'Really, I'm not interested.' But in her heart of hearts she knew she was.

'Look, all I'm saying is Dex is my friend as well as my boss. In fact, I'm probably the only friend he has. He's a very hard man to get to know. But if you care anything for him you should make the effort, Beth. I don't know what went wrong between you weeks ago, but I do know he's been like a bear with a sore head ever since. He was always a workaholic, but lately he's driving himself to the edge.'

'That has nothing to do with me,' Beth muttered, getting to her feet. 'I'm going back.'

'If you say so.' Bob stood up and took her elbow. 'I don't usually interfere in other people's affairs, and if I've offended you, I'm sorry.'

Arm in arm, they walked back into the villa. The crowd was thinning out and Dex saw them immediately. He strolled over, his grey eyes narrowed on Beth. 'Where the devil have you been?' he snapped.

Beth shrank from the rage in his eyes, but before she could answer he added furiously, 'Not content to flirt with every man you danced with, you have to go outside with one!'

'I wasn't flirting,' she choked, feeling incredibly angry. He hadn't spoken to her all night, hadn't danced with her, and now he had the gall to insult her. 'And I went outside because I was hot.'

'Hot.' His lips twisted in a sneer. 'I can believe that.'

'Dex, come on. The girl was with me, and she was perfectly safe,' Bob intervened.

Dex turned to look at Bob. 'I hope so, for your sake.'
Then, as if realising where he was, seeing the curious
glances of the other guests, Dex straightened his shoulders, his dark face expressionless. 'The boat is leaving
in five minutes, Bob. Be on it.' Looking back at Beth,
he added bluntly, 'As Paul's representative, you stay by
me until we've said goodnight to all the guests.'

Smarting at his angry comments, she raised defiant
eyes to his. 'I am not a child to be ordered around.' Dex
had virtually ignored her all day except to tell her what
to do: 'Get in the car' 'Get in the photograph.' He hadn't
even asked her to dance, she thought, burning with re-
sentment.

'Then stop acting like one and do as you're told,' Dex
drawled hardily.

'No, thank you. I'd rather leave now. I can get the
boat—it won't take me a minute to pack.'

One hand snaked out and closed like a manacle
around her wrist. 'You are not going anywhere. Paul left
you in my charge and you will leave as arranged tomorrow. I will personally escort you off the island.
Understand?'

Beth understood all too well. He couldn't wait to get
rid of her. Her brave notion of accepting the wedding
invitation and stunning Dex with her sophisticated attitude was just that—a notion.

'All right,' she snapped. 'You can let go of my hand.'
And, sticking a smile on her face, she did as he had
commanded.

She stood stiffly beside him and accepted the flowing
tributes, the smiles and handshakes, with the best grace
she could muster. All the time intensely conscious of the
dark, brooding man standing beside her.

'Thank heavens for that,' she murmured under her

breath as the last guest departed. Glancing around the huge reception hall, it crossed her mind that perhaps she should help to clean up, but the caterers were buzzing around clearing everything with remarkable efficiency. She wasn't needed, and her bed beckoned.

'My sentiments exactly,' Dex drawled, and took her arm as she stepped forward. 'How about a nightcap?'

She glanced at him quickly over her shoulder. He had loosened his bow tie and unfastened the first few buttons of his shirt. He was so devilishly attractive; her heart lurched at the sight of him.

'I don't think so. I've had enough.' And she was not just talking about drink. It had suddenly hit her that once the caterers departed she would be virtually alone in the house with Dex, and it did nothing for her peace of mind.

CHAPTER TEN

DEX'S black head inclined towards her. 'As you wish. I will show you to your room.'

'No way,' she said bluntly, placing her hand on his chest to ward him off. She raised her eyes to his. 'I do not need a repeat of last night. Go have your drink.' The heavy pounding of his heart beneath her hand found an echo in her own body, and she trembled from head to toe.

'It is not a drink I need,' Dex said thickly, his eyes glittering down into hers. 'I need to once more strip that seductive suit from you.' With one long finger he traced a line from her collarbone down the vee of her jacket to slide along the soft curve of her breast. 'And lose myself in your body. Unlike you, I can never have enough,' he drawled, his deep, husky voice playing on her over-sensitive nerves.

Beth was struck dumb. She stared up at him, her fingers shaking on his chest, her nipples hardening against the fine fabric of her top in shameful arousal. She was mesmerised by the smouldering desire in his silver eyes. For a long moment she simply stared, torn between the desire to know once more the pleasure of his possession and the certain knowledge that she meant little or nothing to him.

Would it be so wrong? she asked herself. To have one more night in his arms? She loved him even though he didn't deserve her love, didn't want it.

A loud crash brought her back to her senses with a jolt. One of the caterers had dropped a tray of glasses. Beth quickly snatched her hand back from his chest and, spinning on her heel, dashed upstairs. She only paused for breath when she was safely in her bedroom with the door locked behind her.

Thank God for a clumsy waiter! Another second and she would have slid her arms around Dex and been his for the taking, Beth bleakly admitted to herself. Stripping off her clothes, she showered and slipped on her white cotton nightie. She was exhausted, but too agitated too sleep, her body aching with frustration. Disgusted with herself, she methodically set about packing her weekend case. She was leaving in the morning and it would save time. She left out her blue jeans, a cashmere sweater and her navy jacket.

Finally, with nothing left to do, she got into bed. But sleep was elusive. She relived the events of the past two days in her head.

Her harmless walk with Paul and Dex's violent re-action had been terrifying. But had it only been on behalf of his sister, or could he possibly have been a little bit jealous of Beth herself? The thought brought solace to her bruised heart. And then later, in this room, Dex had reminded her she hadn't called him when he'd tried to blackmail her. She suddenly realised Dex had still not known Paul was her godfather, so at any time in the past two weeks he could have got Mike fired from his job, and yet he had not done it. Which proved Dex was not all bad...

Today he had hardly spoken to her, and yet he had warned her off Bob quite emphatically. Dex no longer had any need to pretend he liked her, so why warn her about Bob? Unless he was jealous. She was clutching at straws, she knew. But then again, Bob was convinced Dex *did* like her. He had told her in the garden Dex was a hard man to know, and that if she cared anything at all for him it was up to her to make the effort.

Bob's revelation about Dex's ex-wife went a long way to explain Dex's paranoid reaction when he'd thought Beth was going out with Paul, his constant assumption that Beth wanted an older man. Even on their picnic in the New Forest he had hinted as much.

And tonight, when he had asked her to have a drink with him and then quite deliberately tried to... She felt the heat rise in her face and she turned to lie flat on her back. She heard again in her mind his deep velvet voice declare he could not get enough and swallowed hard. If only he knew... She was quite desperate for him. But the difference between them was that Dex wanted her, but she loved him.

What kind of love was it, though, she asked herself, if she didn't dare admit it? She had been quite prepared to swallow her pride for Mike, her stepbrother. Surely she could do at least as much for the man she loved. Dex had once said he liked her honesty. Tomorrow she would be honest and tell Dex how she felt. After all, what was the worst that could happen? He could laugh in her face and tell her to get lost. But after tomorrow she was unlikely to see him again anyway. She had nothing to lose...

A banging on the door woke Beth. She groaned and rolled over.

'Beth, open the door.'

She scrambled out of bed and shot across the room to

turn the key in the lock. The door swung open and she had to jump back as Dex marched in carrying a tray in one hand bearing a coffee pot and cup plus fresh bread rolls and various jams.

Mindful of her decision last night, Beth looked up at him, a tentative smile curving the corners of her wide mouth. This morning he was casually dressed, in well-worn blue jeans and a white sweater that contrasted starkly with his dark good looks. Tearing her eyes away from his powerful body, she looked at the tray he carried. 'For me? Thank you,' she said softly. 'But you needn't have bothered. I...' She'd been going to say she could have eaten downstairs, but didn't get the chance.

'Yes, I did. My housekeeper has already called you once and she is far too old to be running up and down stairs for the likes of you.' His grey eyes scrutinised her slender form with a contempt that made her feel she was naked, lingering on the thrust of her breasts and then down to where her nightie ended mid-thigh before he strolled over to the bedside table and slammed the tray down.

'I'm sorry. I didn't realise.' Beth was trying to stay calm, but his obvious black mood was not helping.

'So you should be.' Dex swung back and walked towards the door. 'You certainly have a penchant for over-sleeping. Obviously you're not bothered by a conscience.'

'Now wait a minute!' Beth exclaimed, her small chin jutting belligerently. She might have been prepared to swallow her pride last night, but she was fast going off the idea as she stared at Dex's frowning face.

'You don't have a minute. It is ten o'clock.'

Beth's eyes widened in horror. 'Oh, my God!' Her plane departed from Naples at twelve forty-five.

'Exactly. I want you out of here in twenty minutes.' And he slammed out of the room.

Beth paused for a moment, her head bowed and her long auburn hair falling like a curtain on either side of her face. So much for Bob's idea that Dex might care for her. He couldn't wait to get her out of his house and out of his country.

Her lips tightened in disgust with herself. What a fool she was. Brushing the hair from her face, she stalked over to the bed, poured herself a cup of coffee and drank it, and then determinedly set about getting ready. She would show the arrogant pig just how fast she could be!

In a matter of minutes she was washed and dressed in jeans, sweater and jacket, thanking the foresight that had made her pack her case last night. She scraped her hair back and tied it with a scarf, flung her shoulder bag over her shoulder picked up her case and walked downstairs. All in the space of ten minutes.

Dex appeared from the drawing room door. His steely eyes swept over her and his lips curved in a grimace. 'You're ready. Good. I'll go and collect your luggage. Wait here.'

'This *is* my luggage,' she said curtly, indicating her one small weekend case.

His dark brows rose in astonishment. 'Amazing—a woman who travels light.' Striding over to her, he took the case from her nerveless fingers and headed for the door. 'Come on, we have no time to waste.'

She followed him out of the house and stopped, looking along the drive. 'Where is the car?' Beth demanded.

The sunshine of the past two days had given way to

grey, overcast skies, with black clouds rumbling along the horizon. She shivered as a cold wind whistled along the headland, and she fastened her jacket.

Dex was halfway across the broad expanse of grass, heading towards the terrace. He gave her a backward glance over his shoulder. 'No car. We are going in my launch.'

'But I came on the ferry.'

Dex stopped and turned around to face her. 'I know. But if Anna had seen fit to inform me you were coming I would have arranged for the launch to collect you.'

'Big deal,' Beth muttered under her breath.

'Hurry up.'

Still muttering, Beth followed Dex down the row upon row of terraces until they reached the jetty. Then she stared. It was not the yacht of yesterday but a twenty-foot speed boat, with a small cabin and wheelhouse, tied up against the dock. The blue sea was almost black, the waves lashing the boat against the side of the wooden structure.

Dex had already jumped on board, but Beth eyed the boat and the sea with dismay. 'Are you sure you know what you're doing?' she demanded flatly.

Dex turned back and, reaching a long arm over the side of the boat, caught her hand in his. 'For heaven's sake, woman, get on the boat and let's go.' He was almost dragging her up the short gangplank.

'The sea looks a bit rough,' she ventured.

'It wasn't an hour ago,' Dex snapped.

Even the weather was her fault now, Beth thought, thoroughly fed up. Stepping into the bottom of the boat, she pulled her hand free from his. 'Well, it is now,' she snapped back, glaring up at him.

His dark brows drew together in a frown of irritation. For once in your life will you stop arguing and do as I tell you? I am going to go up and start the engine—' he gestured with his hand to the wheelhouse '—and when I cry "cast off" all you have to do is slip that rope off that cleat. Understand?' He pointed to where a rope from a capstan on the jetty stretched out to an iron thing on the boat.

'Yes, of course. I'm not a simpleton.' Beth gave him a nasty glance, then looked from Dex to the back of the boat and took a deep breath. What she knew about boats would not cover a postage stamp, but she wasn't going to tell him that. She glanced back and saw he was already at the wheel. Slipping her shoulder bag off her arm, she laid it on a box-like thing and staggered to the back of the boat.

She bent down and tried to get her fingers round the rope. She moved around slightly, to get a better grip.

Dex started the engine and yelled, 'Ready, Beth?'

At the sound of his voice she jerked up, taking the rope with her. The next thing she knew she was flying through the air. She screamed! The rope slipped from her grasp and she hit the water flat on her back.

I'll kill the bastard, was the first thought in her head, and then she swallowed what felt like half the Mediterranean and sank like a stone. Her next thought was survival, as the cold black water closed over her, pressing her down. Kicking out with her feet, she pushed for the surface, but her heavy clothes hampered her. Struggling to hold her breath, she tore at the buttons of her jacket and wriggled out of it. Her lungs felt as if they were bursting as she kicked out again. Finally her head broke the surface of the water, and she took a great

gulp of air before a wave smashed down on her, pushing
her under once more.

Fighting again for the surface, she managed to gasp a
few more breaths of air. She could see the jetty some
ten yards away, and a metal ladder which disappeared
under the water. She might not know much about boats
but she was a good swimmer, and, mentally gritting her
teeth, she struck out for the ladder.

Suddenly an arm shot around her neck, knocking what
little breath she had straight out of her body. Panicking
she struggled wildly, and then she felt a sharp blow, and
nothing more.

Beth's eyelids fluttered, and then she coughed, and
coughed again, water streaming from her mouth. She
groaned and slowly opened her eyes. Her head was
pressed against a broad shoulder and two strong arms
supported her and carried her along. But she was soaked
and frozen to the bone.

'*Grazie a Dio*! You are alive…' Dex's deep voice
echoed in her head. 'Don't try to speak, my love. I have
you safe.'

Her eyes fluttered closed again. She was shaking so
much she couldn't speak, her teeth would not stop chat-
tering and great shudders racked her small frame. She
was vaguely aware of being lowered to her feet, that
gentle hands were stripping off her sweater. She opened
her eyes again. Somehow she was back in her bathroom
and it was Dex who was supporting her, with one arm
around her waist, while with his other hand he was peel-
ing her sodden jeans off her legs.

She tried to lift her hands to resist, but another wave
of shivers convulsed her. Then once more she was lifted
from the floor and suddenly she was being held under a

ascade of water. She flinched, bowing her head as the ot water stung her numb flesh, then gradually some of 1e numbness faded and the warmth of the water began) sink through to her frozen bones.

Also it began to sink into her shocked brain that she vas being supported by two strong bare arms. 'What...?' vas as much as she got out.

'Shh, shh, Beth.' And she was wrapped in a huge uffy towel, and strong hands began to rub her all over. I will take care of you.'

Take care of her! Suddenly it all came back to Beth: 1e boat, the sea—everything. Somehow finding the trength, she slapped his hands away.

'What the hell do you think you're doing?' she cried oarsely, her throat raw from the sea water. And, stag- ering back, she grabbed the towel, wrapped it toga-style nder her arms and knotted it.

'You need to get warm. You've had a severe shock.'

She whipped the tangled mass of her wet hair out of er eyes and lifted her head, and got an even bigger hock. Dex was standing in front of her, water droplets ripping off his black hair onto his broad shoulders, rickling down his muscular chest, his flat belly. She ulped. Her eyes flew wide open and trailed down to the rush of black curls, protecting the beginning of his mas- uline sex, and lower, to his long, muscular legs. He was tark naked.

'You...you...get out,' she squeaked, still shivering rith cold but intensely aware of his magnificent all-male ody.

'This is no time for modesty, Beth. I have to get you varm. You might have hypothermia.'

She was more likely to hyperventilate if he didn't put

something on—and quickly, she thought distractedly glancing wildly around the bathroom, anywhere but at the naked man towering over her. Her eye caught a towel on the rail. 'So might you,' Beth choked, and, reaching out, snagged the towel and shoved it at Dex. 'Here.'

His large hand covered hers and pulled her toward him. Taking the towel from her nerveless fingers, he casually slung it around his hips. 'Your concern is touching, Beth.' He chuckled deep in his throat. 'But seriously, you were in the water a lot longer than I.' Reaching out, he pulled her into the circle of his arms and held her pressed tightly against him. 'Humour, me hmm?' he murmured when she tried to pull free, and he gently stroked her back and buttocks through the towel.

For a long moment Beth gave herself up to the unaccustomed comfort of being held in Dex's arms. Gradually her shivering stopped and a slow warmth spread through her body. Her jaw ached and she cushioned it gently against the hairs on his chest. There was nothing sexual about it. Maybe she just needed the sense of care and protection Dex was offering.

'Better now, sweetheart?' Dex asked, rubbing his chin on the top of her head. 'Come on, let me get you into bed.'

The mention of 'bed' broke through her dazed brain. My God! What was she doing? She was supposed to be on a plane to England. Instead she was standing almost naked in a bathroom...and it was all Dex's fault.

Beth looked up at him. 'You've got to be joking.' She couldn't control her anger. He was smiling down at her. Clad in only a towel, he looked wickedly attractive, and a swift stab of regret pierced her heart, but she quickly vanquished her wayward feelings. 'You bastard.'

The smile left his eyes and his hard face tautened arrogantly. 'Bastard, yes. But I only mentioned bed for you—for warmth. Not for me. I can't help it if you have a one-track mind,' he drawled mockingly, his arms falling away from her.

Free and furious, Beth registered his mocking insult and it was too much for her fragile emotions. 'Why…you…you…supercilious swine. You're crazy…stark, staring mad… First you punch out my godfather, and then you try to drown me. Not content with that, you almost strangle me, and then you knock me out.' The pain in her jaw, she realised, was from when Dex had grabbed her in the water. Rubbing her hand over the bruise, she glared defiantly at Dex. 'What happens next…a knife in the gut?'

She had no idea how incredibly lovely she looked, her green eyes flashing fire, nor how heartbreakingly young and vulnerable, with one of her hands clasping the precarious knot in the towel around her slender body.

Beth was not aware of the fierce tension tautening Dex's large frame, her eyes were suddenly filling with moisture. The after-effects of the traumatic shock she had suffered were catching up with her.

'No knife. But I will love you to death,' Dex said hoarsely. And, catching her by the shoulders, his fingers digging into her flesh, he added urgently, 'If you will only let me, Beth.'

She gazed up at him and saw such anguish, such need in the depths of his silver eyes her heart stopped. She blinked, unable to believe what she was seeing.

'I love you so much, Beth. Please say something, anything,' he demanded, his voice raw with emotion. 'I thought I could let you walk away, but I can't.'

She stared at him. The cold, remote mask he showed the world was gone, and she saw his heart in his eyes. 'You love me,' she murmured. 'You love me!' she exclaimed, her own eyes overflowing with tears of emotion. The impossible had happened.

'Please don't cry, Beth. Please, I never meant to make you cry,' he pleaded. 'As God is my witness, I didn't tip you out of the boat. I asked if you were ready, and you cast off instead. When I saw you in the water I jumped in to save you because I couldn't bear the thought of my life without you. If I was too clumsy, I'm sorry. But carrying you back to the house was the most horrendous walk of my life. I wouldn't hurt you for the world. You must believe that. I love you.'

She lifted her small hand to his face and stroked from his temple down to his jaw. 'I'm not crying because you hurt me.' A wide smile of pure joy lit her lovely face. 'I'm overwhelmed because you love me—as I love you.'

Dex looked deep into her huge green eyes. 'You love me? Since when?' he asked roughly.

'From the first moment I saw you.' Beth stared up at him, and what he saw in her eyes told him she was telling the truth.

He groaned and swept her into his arms, kissing her with a hard, hungry passion. Beth clung to him, her arms around his neck, returning his kiss with equal passion as though between them they could erase the heartache of the past few weeks. The towels fell away, they were naked together, and Dex's hard, aroused body ground against hers. His hands slid down to cup her buttocks and lift her bodily off her feet.

Involuntarily Beth locked her legs around him, afraid to fall, then gasped as the hard length of him nudged against the delta of her thighs. His head bent to her breasts and he took one into his mouth and suckled fiercely. Beth whimpered, her arms tightening around his neck as he did the same to the other one.

He lifted his head and his fierce silver eyes caught and held hers. 'I have loved you from the first time I saw you, too,' he growled, deep in his throat, and thrust up into her. She cried out, her eyes widening the second he took possession of her.

It was a wild, savagely quick coupling. Dex's taut face became a dark blur, and Beth gave herself up to the wild ride until with a hoarse cry Dex shuddered violently, spilling his seed inside her, and she convulsed around him.

Dex held her for a long moment as shudder after shudder racked his great body. Beth felt the lingering spasms in every nerve-ending of her body. Finally Dex lowered her slowly to the floor, and if he had not been holding her she would have collapsed at his feet. Her legs were shaking, her whole body shook...

'Hell! What am I thinking of?' Dex swore hoarsely, staring down into her flushed face. 'I am an insensitive jerk.' And, swinging her up in his arms, he carried her through to the bedroom and placed her gently on the bed.

When he would have stood up, Beth curled her hand around the back of his neck. 'So long as you are *my* jerk,' she prompted, a questioning light in her green eyes. The last few minutes had left her dazed and awed by the wonder and power of her lover. But did it mean the miracle had happened and Dex really loved her?

'Always and for ever,' Dex vowed, lowering his long body over her. His hands palmed either side of her head

and he kissed her slowly, gently, with aching tenderness
'But now, my love…' He rolled to one side and curved
his arm firmly around her, so they were lying side by
side, and with his other hand pulled the coverlet over
them. He leaned over her. 'Now you need to rest.' He
gently pushed back a strand of damp hair from her brow
and stared down at her, the banked-down passion in his
silver eyes firmly controlled. 'You could catch cold,
pneumonia, and now I have you I am taking no chances
on losing you again.'

She wanted to believe him, but still a nagging doubt
haunted her. 'You're not just saying that because you
feel guilty about…about everything?' she asked, stam-
mering over the words.

'Making love to you so desperately you mean?' He
favoured her with an ironic look.

'I…' She blushed. 'I didn't know you could make
love like that. Standing, I mean, and so hot and fast…'

'There is a lot you don't know about love, and I am
going to spend my life teaching you,' he said, gently
outlining her lips with his finger. 'Before, in the bathroom, I could not have stopped myself, and neither could
you. No matter what the differences between us, there
was never any doubt from the first time I kissed you that
the chemistry between us was electric.'

'In the casino,' Beth said softly, remembering. 'You
were angry because Paul was there and I spoke to him.'

Dex sighed. 'For that I do feel guilty.'

'You only took me out because of Paul and Anna,'
Beth said reflectively. 'So when…?' She hesitated.
'When did you fall in love with me?' It was the one
question she desperately wanted the answer to.

'With hindsight, probably from that night. I kissed you and went up in flames.'

'Don't lie to me, Dex,' Beth said quietly. 'We both know that isn't true.'

'True? What is truth?' Dex demanded, looking into her worried eyes. 'You want the truth—I will give it to you. You know I have been married before, that my wife left me for an older, richer man?'

'That must have been hard.'

'Not really. I had long since stopped loving her—if I ever did. She was the first woman I had sex with, so I married her. She then proceeded to dole out her favours—very occasionally, and only after I had presented her with a suitably expensive piece of jewellery. She was a mercenary, frigid bitch, but it took me five years to realise it.'

Beth could her the anger in his voice. 'I'm sorry. You don't have to talk about it...'

'Yes, I do, Beth, because she coloured my view of women for years. Until I met you I had never been out with the same woman more than a couple of times. I am not proud of how I have lived my life, I admit, but when I met you I had no intention of changing.' He tenderly smoothed her hair down the side of her head, and dropped a soft kiss on her brow.

'But with you I met my Waterloo, Beth, darling. I kept telling myself I was seeing you to keep you away from Paul for Anna's sake, but I think I knew deep down I loved you. I vowed after my divorce I would never give another woman a piece of jewellery, and yet I found myself quite happily standing in a jeweller's shop, picking out a ring for you. The day after we got engaged and I went to New York I finally admitted to myself I loved you. A week in your company and I missed you so badly I wanted to phone you a dozen times a day.'

'You didn't, though,' Beth said, remembering her own doubts at the time. 'You didn't even tell me where you lived, about this house... Did you share it with your wife?' She still had doubts, she realised.

'The villa was built after my divorce, and, no, I didn't phone you as I wanted to. And then I got back to England, and the conversation you overheard. Well, it was my last-ditch attempt to pretend I was not desperately in love with you. I made myself have a drink with Bob. Bob knows me well, and I think he guessed the truth when I told him I had given you an engagement ring. I said the things I did to him because I was on the defensive, but in my heart I knew I wanted you and I was going to marry you.' His grey eyes hardened. 'I made myself delay seeing you only to discover you were out. Then you kept me waiting for hours and gave me my marching orders.'

She could hear the underlying fury in his tone. 'Only because I thought you were using me,' she responded, and gently stroked her fingers through the crisp hair on his broad chest. He caught her hand in his and placed it around his waist, one long leg moving restlessly against her thigh.

'What price truth, then, Beth? You could have told me.'

'Pride,' Beth said sadly. 'Plain pride. I thought, why should I tell you about Paul and put you and your sister out of your misery? It was nothing to do with me. And later, well...you were so angry...'

'Later...' Dex sighed, a deep frown creasing his brow. 'I behaved like an animal. Afterwards I stood in that tiny bathroom of yours for ages, afraid to come out, afraid to face you. And then you said I'd forced you, and, heaven help me, I still wonder. Can you ever forgive me for that night, Beth?'

How could she have let him think that? Especially now she knew how his ex-wife had treated him. 'Oh, Dex!' She stroked her hand up his back. 'There was nothing to forgive. I'm ashamed to admit I only said that because I was shocked at how much I wanted you and how much I—well…' She looked away, still shy even though they had been as close as it was possible for two people to be.

'Well, what?' He caught her chin and turned her back to face him, his silver eyes boring into hers.

'How much I enjoyed—no, loved what you did to me. Then I felt shocked, ashamed at my own reaction, and I took it out on you.'

A slow smile of pure male pride curved his sensuous mouth. 'And I took it out on you, in a way. I resented the fact that I had fallen in love with you, but in my conceit I thought you would be forever grateful I was going to marry you. My pride was shattered when you had the nerve to jilt me.'

'But you came back,' Beth said breathlessly as his hand trailed down from her breast and settled low on her stomach. 'Hallowe'en night. And you tried to blackmail me.'

'Ah, yes, the party,' Dex drawled huskily, lowering his head and brushing her lips with his. 'Seeing you in that cat costume has caused me more erotic dreams than I dare think about.'

'You wouldn't really have cost Mike his job?' Beth asked, just as he was about to kiss her again.

'I can't blame you for asking, but, no, I would never do anything that would harm you. It was the last, desperate try of a man crazy with love but not prepared to admit it. When you didn't call the next morning, I rang you.'

'That's right,' Beth realised. 'The phone woke me up.' But there was still something she didn't understand. 'If you knew you loved me, why were you so furious with me on Friday night?'

'On Friday I had just flown in from New York. Anna had not seen fit to tell me anything about the wedding, simply the time and place, and I arrived to see you kissing Paul. I yelled at you because I was mad with jealousy, and then when you explained I felt a complete fool. I hoped to talk to you later that night, try and start afresh.'

'I did think you looked a bit nervous when you came into my bedroom. This room.' She smiled up at him.

'You are so innocent, Beth.' His hand slid from her stomach to stroke back up her body and settle softly over one breast. Not for much longer, if Dex has his way, Beth thought, as her nipple hardened beneath his palm and she moved her hips restlessly from side to side.

He chuckled, his thumb flicking the nub of her breast. 'I can laugh now. But have you any idea what it does to a man's ego to have the woman he loves tell him she overslept? I spent the whole night at my hotel unable to sleep, waiting to hear your answer. And you overslept!'

'The answer was no, anyway,' she murmured, and nestled closer to his hard frame, rubbing one of her shapely legs against his muscular hair-covered one.

'I guessed as much. You're not the type of woman to

be bullied into anything,' he opined with an ironic smile. 'And God knows, I've tried.'

'I noticed,' she teased, and then frowned. 'But yesterday you ignored me almost all day.'

'Ignored you!' Dex grinned, his silver eyes gleaming with wicked delight. 'My god, Beth, I didn't dare look at you. When I saw you in the red suit again, my body reacted much the same way as it is now.' He flung a long leg over her slim hips and made her vitally aware of his aroused state.

'I could barely walk straight all day. I wanted to kill Bob for talking to you, but I didn't dare stay beside you myself. And as for dancing with you, I couldn't trust myself not to have you on the dance floor.'

'Dex, that's terrible!' She laughed, finally believing this proud, handsome man did love her.

He rolled over her completely. 'Truthfully, Beth, I resented the way you made me feel. I don't like to be out of control. And this morning, when you slept in again, after I'd had another sleepless night, I was furious. I thought, why waste my time yearning for a girl who obviously cares so little she doesn't lose so much as a minute's sleep over me? But when I saw you in the sea... Pride, conditioning—nothing mattered but that I told you how I feel. I love you and I want you to marry me. And you still haven't answered.'

'Yes,' she murmured, and answered him in the most convincing way. She slipped one hand around his neck as her other hand traced down over his hip and around his thigh.

Dex groaned and covered her mouth with his. This time it was a long, slow loving, and at the end Beth opened her eyes and watched his dark face contort in rigid lines of ecstasy before she was swept along in a torrent of sensations, her eyes closing, and she cried out as they reached the ultimate release together.

'Are you all right?'

She heard his voice and slowly opened her eyes. She could feel his heart slamming against his chest where he lay on top of her, her own equally as erratic. 'I'm...I'm fine,' she whispered, and, lifting her hand, she pushed back the errant black curl from his damp brow.

His grey eyes were almost black as they held hers. 'The rare times I could sleep I used to dream of you like this,' he rasped. 'Your glorious hair spread across my pillow, your luscious body beneath mine. But my dreams came nowhere near the reality, Beth.' He gently rubbed his mouth against hers. 'I want you to know it has never been like this for me before...ever...'

Beth wrapped her arms around him and hugged him to her. 'I'm glad,' she sighed.

'You are the only woman in the world for me and I will cherish you to my dying day. Understand?' Dex said, almost fiercely.

So typical of Dex, Beth thought, rejoicing in his avowal of love. Even when he was at his most vulnerable, sated with love and laying his heart at her feet, the arrogant, powerful man still shone through. She smiled lazily up at him. 'I understand,' she said demurely, and kissed him.

Dex rolled over and pulled her gently into his arms. 'Are you warm enough?'

Beth laughed out loud. 'If I was any hotter the sheets would catch fire and your housekeeper...' She sat up. 'Oh, my God. It's the middle of the day—anyone could

walk in.' Her eyes slid down over his naked body and
she blushed.

'Don't panic. The housekeeper and her son always
have Sunday afternoon off.' Dex chuckled, amused by
her embarrassment at his nudity.

'I've missed my plane. I have to go to work tomorrow.' In the euphoria of discovering Dex loved her, Beth
had forgotten the more mundane aspects of life.

'Forget it.' Dex caught her around the waist and
pulled her down on top of him. 'You don't have to work
any more; you're going to be my wife.'

'A lady of leisure?' Beth queried. 'I don't think I'd
like that,' she told him seriously, resting her arms on his
chest and staring down at him.

'Remember the first time I visited your apartment?'

'What has that got to do with anything?' Beth asked.
He wasn't taking her desire to work seriously.

'You have a computer for your graphic art, but you
also keep a drawing board. Maybe you are more like
your father than you know. I could convert one of the
rooms here into a studio for you. Think about it, Beth.
Given a choice, which do you prefer? Hands-on art or
sitting at a computer?'

'You're right…you know me so well.' She looked
down into his eyes and he grinned, his hands sliding
down over her bottom.

'And now I'm going to know you again,' he drawled
throatily. And he did…

Eighteen months later, the priest and a group of people
stood outside the little church on the Isle of Capri in the
spring sunshine.

'If they're not here in the next five minutes it will be

too late. I have another baptism at ten-thirty,' the priest told Mr Morris—who was holding his own one-year-old boy in his arms—and Mrs Morris, the prospective godparents.

A white Mercedes drew up with a squeal of brakes. Dexter and Bethany Giordanni got out, Dex carrying a small infant in his arms. They raced up to the church door, Beth very red-faced, her husband suffering from no such embarrassment.

'What happened to you, Dexter? You're twenty minutes late for your child's christening,' Anna reprimanded her brother.

Dex turned, looking at Beth, his silver eyes brilliant with reminiscent pleasure. Beth blushed even redder and Dex, with a wicked wink, turned back to his sister and said, 'We overslept.' And, with his baby girl in one arm and his other arm around his wife, he swept past an open-mouthed Anna into the church...

HARLEQUIN PRESENTS®

Penny Jordan!

THE CRIGHTONS

are back!

This breathtaking family saga continues.

Enter
The Perfect Lover
Harlequin Presents® #2025, May 1999

In this fantastic new stand-alone novel,
Louise Crighton finds herself working with
Gareth Simmonds, the man with whom she'd
once shared a whirlwind holiday romance....

Available wherever Harlequin books are sold.

HARLEQUIN®
Makes any time special ™

HARLEQUIN ✦ PRESENTS®

THE BARONS

One sister, three brothers— who will inherit, and will they all find lovers?

Jonas is approaching his eighty-fifth birthday, and he's decided it's time to choose the heir of his sprawling ranch, Espada. He has three ruggedly good-looking sons, Gage, Travis and Slade, and a beautiful stepdaughter, Caitlin.

Who will receive Baron's bequest? As the Baron brothers and their sister discover, there's more at stake than Espada. For love also has its part to play in deciding their futures....

Enjoy Gage's story:
Marriage on the Edge
Harlequin Presents #2027, May 1999

And in August, get to know Travis a whole lot better in
More than a Mistress
Harlequin Presents #2045

Available wherever Harlequin books are sold.

✦ HARLEQUIN®
*M*akes any time special ™

Coming Next Month

 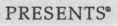

THE BEST HAS JUST GOTTEN BETTER!

#2031 WEDDED BLISS Penny Jordan & Carole Mortimer
Two complete stories in one book to celebrate Harlequin's
50th anniversary.

THEY'RE WED AGAIN! Penny Jordan
Belle Crawford found herself seated next to her ex-husband
Luc at a wedding. They'd been divorced for seven years so
everyone expected fireworks—and there were...fireworks
sparked by passion!

THE MAN SHE'LL MARRY Carole Mortimer
Merry Baker had been cruelly jilted by the father of her child
eighteen years ago, so she'd never really considered men or
marriage. But after meeting handsome Zack Kingston she had
to change her mind....

#2032 HER GUILTY SECRET Anne Mather
Alex's life had fallen apart when his wife died, and he'd lost
custody of his baby daughter. Now he was suspicious of his
gorgeous new employee, Kate Hughes. Was she involved with
his fight to get his daughter back?

#2033 THE PRICE OF A BRIDE Michelle Reid
Mia agreed to marry millionaire Alexander Doumas so that
both he and her father would gain from the deal. But how
could Mia's real reason for marrying Alex be kept a secret
when she shared such passion with him every night?

#2034 ACCIDENTAL BABY Kim Lawrence
To Jo, gorgeous Liam Rafferty was simply her best friend.
Until one night they accidentally got too close—and Jo
found herself pregnant! Unexpectedly, Liam insisted on
marriage....

#2035 THE GROOM'S REVENGE Kate Walker
India had been about to say "I do" when Aidan, the fiancé
she loved and desired, accused her of being a gold digger
and promptly jilted her. Now Aidan was back wanting
revenge: he'd help India's family, but for a price—India....

#2036 SLEEPING WITH THE BOSS Cathy Williams
Victor Temple worked with his assistant Alice, all day, every
day. Their relationship had always been strictly business—
until now. Suddenly Victor had seen behind her neat
professional disguise and found the real, passionate Alice....